Samantha cap... star and desce...

Mark gripped her protectively around the waist and lifted her from the last step to slide her down the length of his body.

"I like the way that feels." She draped her arms over his shoulders. "Think anyone would notice if we made the most of it?"

Clearing his throat, Mark dipped his head toward their audience of infants arrayed in carriers around the tree. "Let's keep this G-rated."

Sam poked him in the ribs. "All right, then. Stand back."

The tree glowed with a display of treasures transformed into fairy gifts. Outside, twilight had fallen, which only intensified the brilliance inside.

"Their first Christmas tree," she said.

One of the babies cooed appreciatively, clueless that they'd also just worked their first Christmas miracle.

Dear Reader,

A fiery advocate for the children she treats, pediatrician Samantha Forrest has postponed having children of her own. Now, to her dismay, she learns that she'll probably never be able to have any. When circumstances drop a set of adorable triplets into her lap, how can she resist?

Dr. Mark Rayburn, administrator of Safe Harbor Medical Center, is happy living alone, free from the family turmoil he grew up with. But when Samantha's headstrong leap into motherhood lands her in hot water, he pitches in...even at the risk of getting burned.

These two opposites love to squabble and throw obstacles in each other's paths...and they're about to discover how many other things they love to do together, too.

Happy reading!

Best wishes,

Jacqueline Diamond

www.jacquelinediamond.com

The Holiday Triplets
JACQUELINE DIAMOND

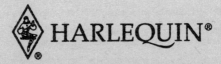

HARLEQUIN®

TORONTO • NEW YORK • LONDON
AMSTERDAM • PARIS • SYDNEY • HAMBURG
STOCKHOLM • ATHENS • TOKYO • MILAN • MADRID
PRAGUE • WARSAW • BUDAPEST • AUCKLAND

Recycling programs
for this product may
not exist in your area.

ISBN-13: 978-0-373-75339-0

THE HOLIDAY TRIPLETS

Copyright © 2010 by Jackie Hyman

This edition published by arrangement with Harlequin Books S.A.

For questions and comments about the quality of this book
please contact us at Customer_eCare@Harlequin.ca

® and TM are trademarks of the publisher. Trademarks indicated with
® are registered in the United States Patent and Trademark Office, the
Canadian Trade Marks Office and in other countries.

www.eHarlequin.com

Printed in U.S.A.

ABOUT THE AUTHOR

Growing up as the daughter of a doctor, Jacqueline Diamond—author of more than 80 novels—developed an appreciation for the demands and rewards of the medical profession. Most of all, she understands that doctors are just people with a special gift and dedication, who fall in love and wrestle with family issues like everyone else. She's also the daughter of internationally renowned ceramic sculptor Sylvia Hyman. You can learn more about Jackie and see some of her mother's artwork at www.jacquelinediamond.com. If you write Jackie at jdiamondfriends@yahoo.com, she'll be happy to add you to her email list.

Books by Jacqueline Diamond

HARLEQUIN AMERICAN ROMANCE

For Arthur Gunzberg on his 99th birthday

Chapter One

On a Wednesday morning in early December, Dr. Mark Rayburn set out on foot from his house, enjoying the crisp ocean breeze through the palm trees but already eagerly anticipating his arrival at Safe Harbor Medical Center.

This was *his* hospital.

He'd bought a house four blocks away to avoid southern California's infamously long commutes and also because he liked being able to drop in frequently at the center, whether at night or early in the morning or on holidays. Long hours weren't a burden; they were a privilege.

He didn't want or need a family, because he already had one. As administrator, he guided and nudged and cheered for his staff. As an obstetrician, he nurtured mothers and helped babies take their miraculous first breath. And now he had a chance to make a real difference in the world, to help even more women and families. What could be better than that?

At the edge of the medical center, Mark paused to admire the hospital's clean lines and curving, window-lined wings. The six-story structure anchored a complex that included a medical office building, a parking garage and a dental building that the hospital's corporate owner was acquiring to turn into a fertility center.

This was his dream, the reason he'd become an admini-

strator and moved from Florida to California. Soon, he'd
be assembling a world-class team of doctors and support
staff so that even more families could turn their dreams
into reality.

Still, excited as he was about the fertility center plans,
he never slighted the less showy part of his domain. Sauntering past a profusion of birds-of-paradise plants and
calla lilies, Mark bypassed the staff entrance and walked
through the wide central doors into the lobby. Coming
in this way helped him stay in touch with what ordinary
patients experienced.

Today, the place glittered with holiday spirit. Busy elves
from the Hospital Guild Auxiliary had festooned the lobby
with twinkling white lights and Santa faces beaming from
wreaths. To one side, gingerbread men and miniature por-
celain baby dolls dangled from a nonallergenic tree.

Nostalgia and painful memories twisted inside Mark.
Brushing aside the ghosts of Christmases past, he quickened the pace of his informal patrol.

At a little past 7:00 a.m., the gift shop hadn't opened
yet, but the clatter of breakfast dishes echoed from the
nearby cafeteria. As he strode along a corridor, he heard
an instructor exhorting an aerobics class to greater exer-
tions in the workout room, and paused to let an orderly
pass with a cart full of medications.

"Hey, Dr. Rayburn." The young man gave him an easy
grin.

"Good morning, Bob." Mark made a point of remembering his staff's names.

He had a lot of them rattling around in his brain as he
mounted the stairs. Names of doctors, nurses, lab techs,
secretaries and, of course, patients. Even though he'd been
an administrator for the last five of his thirty-seven years,

including two here at Safe Harbor, he still found time to provide one-on-one treatment.

On the third floor, he stopped by labor and delivery to greet the hardworking nurses and find out how his maternity patients were doing. He'd delivered five babies yesterday, including triplets born to a young mom.

"Everyone's fine." His nurse, Lori Ross, updated him on the essentials. Two of the three new mothers would be going home today, while the triplets' mom, Candy Alarcon, needed another day or so to recuperate from her cesarean section. "The pediatrician's talking to her now."

"Dr. Sellers?" Neonatologist Jared Sellers had examined the babies in the delivery room. He also happened to be Lori's ex-fiancé, and therefore a touchy subject.

"Uh, no." She gave him a shaky smile. "Dr. Forrest."

"Ah."

You couldn't in all fairness describe Samantha Forrest as a thorn in his side, Mark reflected as he headed toward the patients' rooms. He valued her dedication and her passion for social justice. The problem was that she tended to be a bit of a drama queen.

As did Candy, an unmarried nineteen-year-old whom Samantha had counseled through a volunteer program. That made them an unpredictable combination.

To give them a chance to talk freely, Mark decided to visit his other two patients first.

"No one said this was going to be easy," Samantha told the young woman in the bed. "I just don't want you to look back in ten or twenty years and ask, why did I let them go? You've been so eager to keep them until now. It's normal to have second thoughts."

Candy's bow-shaped mouth twisted. Curly hair framed a pretty face that hid the insecurities of a girl who'd grown up alternately indulged and abandoned by troubled parents. "Honestly, Dr. Forrest, I do want to be a good mother. But I feel overwhelmed. And one of them's got that…that thing on her face."

"It's called a port-wine stain." Sam wished she had baby Connie and her sister and brother in the room to remind Candy of how adorable they were, but, as a precaution, they were still being monitored in the intermediate-care nursery. As for the purplish blotch on Connie's cheek, it was superficial rather than an indication of any serious syndrome. "We can treat that with lasers, and if it doesn't completely go away, she can cover it with makeup when she's older."

"It might not go away?" Candy asked anxiously.

"Sometimes a trace remains. But your babies are healthy. That's a blessing, especially with triplets."

Since meeting the young mother months ago at a teen moms' support group that Sam had organized, she'd arranged for prenatal treatment and put Candy in touch with a nonprofit agency that would provide temporary nursing care after the infants went home. In addition, a local charity had pledged to collect baby supplies and used cribs. Sam had spent hours calling and organizing to arrange it all, but it was worth the effort to get this family off to a good start.

"My boyfriend says she's ugly. I thought he'd love them the way I do." Candy drooped against the pillow.

Samantha winced. "Give Jon time. He's falling in love with them already." The previous night at the nursery, she could have sworn the young man's face had lit with pride as he surveyed his children.

"He imagined he could land us a reality TV show." The girl's eyes teared up. "Isn't that ridiculous? I told him we'd need at least eight babies to do that."

"And even then, it wouldn't be in their best interest." Sam tried to cover her dismay. How could people exploit their children? When she had kids of her own, she planned to treasure and protect them with every ounce of her strength.

If I ever have kids. But that was neither here nor there. At the moment, her pediatric patients and the young mothers she nurtured came first with Sam. "Maybe he was kidding."

"I doubt it. He's so immature!" Candy blew out a long breath. "I believed we were in love and he'd marry me once I got pregnant, but he keeps putting it off."

"He'll come around." Samantha searched for a positive angle. "Your mom offered to pitch in, too."

"Yeah, but her idea of pitching in is babysitting once a month. She works awfully hard." The new grandma worked as a waitress, a job that took a heavy physical toll. "And she just hooked up with a new guy. Jerry's not into babies."

"I didn't know that." Sam had only met the grandmother briefly. "The service will be sending aides for the first few months."

"What about after that?" Candy waved her hands helplessly. "My dad was never around. I don't want my kids to grow up that way, too."

Samantha leaned forward. "You have to fight for what matters, Candy. I don't mean to push you into anything you aren't ready for, but if you give up too easily, you might regret it for the rest of your life."

When the stakes were high, you couldn't back down. As a teenager, Sam had nearly given up the most important battle of her life. Thank goodness, with her family's support, she'd rallied. Since then, she'd made it her mission to give others a boost at crucial moments in *their* lives.

Yet, for a moment, she wondered if she'd gone too far. The last thing Sam wanted was to impose her values and dreams on this young woman.

Suddenly a smile brightened Candy's face. "You know what the other girls call you? Fightin' Sam. I'm glad to have you in my corner."

Relieved, Samantha pushed her doubts aside. "That's where you'll find me, all right."

Someone tapped at the open door. Sam didn't have to turn to identify the visitor; she simply inhaled the dangerously thrilling scent of Mark Rayburn's aftershave lotion.

As she listened to Candy's greeting and Mark's deep-voiced answer, Sam kept her face averted so Mark couldn't see her telltale flushed cheeks. Despite her body's traitorous response, she had no intention of letting this man guess how attractive she found him.

In control again, she got to her feet. "Good morning, Mark."

Dark eyes swept her, sending prickles along Samantha's skin. Beneath his white coat, the powerful physique of a former football player loomed in her path. "Good to see you." As if they didn't run into each other practically every day.

Run into each other, and butt heads, and wage polite warfare. Although a fine doctor and an able administrator, Mark Rayburn stood for authority and the bottom line. Which, all too often, made him an obstacle in Samantha's path.

"I'll wait outside till you're done," she said.

His thick eyebrows drew up. "Why wait? Don't you have patients to see?"

"Yes, but there's something I need to run by you."

There was no mistaking the wariness in his expression. "Of course."

With a farewell wave to Candy, Sam went out. She might have a tight schedule, but she never neglected the things that really mattered.

THE INCISION WAS HEALING WELL, and the patient showed no sign of infection. Although Mark lingered for a few minutes after the exam to discuss anything troubling Candy, she insisted she was fine. He left her with a promise to send in the nurse to help her get out of bed. The sooner she started moving, the faster she'd recover.

Triplets. Caring for them would be a huge undertaking for any woman, and especially for this young lady. While he wished her every success, he hoped Samantha hadn't overly influenced Candy's decision to keep them.

In the corridor, he found Sam talking intently with Lori. Just his luck that the two women had become fast friends. So far, they hadn't ganged up on him, though.

As soon as she spotted him, Samantha excused herself. Without prompting, the nurse went in to check on Candy, while Mark pulled off the white coat he'd thrown over his suit.

"Mind climbing the stairs as we talk?" he asked. Although Samantha saw her regular patients in the adjacent office building, she also served as chief of the pediatrics department, which was located on the next floor up. At this early hour, no doubt she planned to make the rounds of her hospitalized patients on that floor.

"Suits me." Her long legs matched his stride easily. Only a few inches shorter than his six-foot height, she had golden hair that, today, swept in waves to her shoulders. He was glad she hadn't stuck it back with a clip or pulled it into a ponytail as she often did.

"What can I do for you?" Mark held the door to the staircase.

"Christmas." She breezed past.

That single word brought back his earlier troubled mood. *His mother and father arguing...Mom drinking some 90-proof concoction she claimed was eggnog... stumbling and knocking over the tree, ripping the string of lights out of the socket...*

Mark searched for a happier memory when he and his sister, Bryn, were little. Piles of gifts from their physician father, a dinner table laden with treats in their Miami home. He preferred those images to the darker ones from his teen years, when it had fallen to him to dry Bryn's tears and sometimes his mother's, too.

"Yes?" He hoped Sam wasn't about to issue an invitation, because he planned to spend this holiday, like most, either working or playing golf. Probably both.

"I got a great idea last night. I'm going to stage an open-house fundraiser for the counseling clinic on Christmas Day."

As she mounted the stairs ahead of him, Mark admired the feminine sway of her body in tailored trousers and a cherry-colored blouse. Still, that didn't mean he had to endorse her latest scheme.

"Most people have plans for Christmas." Launching the grassroots counseling clinic might be *her* pet project, but she could hardly expect the rest of the world to abandon their traditions. "Why not hold it the weekend before?"

"Everybody throws parties then. Besides, did you know Christmas is one of the slowest news days of the year? We'll get much better media coverage." Her voice drifted back.

Mark stifled a groan. If there was anything Safe Harbor didn't lack, it was media coverage.

A few months earlier, a reporter had stirred up a storm by implying that the hospital had a special connection to California's Safe Haven law, which allowed mothers to surrender newborns safely without legal repercussions. As a result, young moms had showed up in record numbers, babes in their arms and news cameras dogging their every move.

The furor had died down at last, but not before Samantha managed to turn the negative publicity into the realization of a dream. With the claim that she wanted to help prevent future relinquishments, she'd persuaded the hospital's owner, a corporation based in Kentucky, to turn over a large office suite for her to use as a counseling clinic for women and families. As if she didn't already have enough volunteer work to do with the teen support group she counseled—but Sam never seemed to run short of energy.

Since then, donations had enabled the Edward Serra Memorial Clinic to acquire furnishings, a computer system, a handful of volunteer peer counselors and the beginnings of an endowment. Not nearly enough to provide paid staff, however.

Hence this latest proposal, he presumed. While Mark supported the clinic's mission, he considered it peripheral to the hospital's central purpose. Plus, it was always risky to let Samantha speak to the press. She had a gift for stirring up controversy.

"We've discussed this before," he reminded her as they reached the fourth floor landing. "To put the clinic on a solid financial footing, you can't rely on nickel-and-dime contributions. You need major corporate sponsors."

"Mark!" She turned so abruptly he nearly ran into her. "How can I attract sponsors without publicity?"

He'd always appreciated her slim, athletic figure, but

rarely had been this close. When she tossed back her blond mane, Mark had to drag his brain back to their conversation.

"Through working quietly behind the scenes. Cultivating contacts. Making presentations." That was how the business world operated.

Sam remained planted one step above him. Unless Mark bodily shifted her aside, he was trapped. And he wasn't eager to put his hands on her body. Actually, he was, but he shouldn't be.

"I am *not* going to spend Christmas assembling a PowerPoint presentation, I'm going to spend it throwing a party! Since I can't celebrate with my parents in Mexico—" both doctors, they ran a charity clinic south of the border "—let's hold a fiesta here. Piñatas, colorful paper flowers and spicy food."

"It does sound like fun," Mark reluctantly agreed.

Samantha dropped her hands to his shoulders, her face inches from his, and teased him with a smile. If he didn't know her better, he might suspect her of flirting. "It will be."

He'd better concede the point before he did something insane, like kiss her in the stairwell. "I'll authorize additional security and cleaning, and I'm sure our public relations staff will be glad to spread the word. But you'll have to come up with the food and entertainment budget."

She bit her lower lip, her brain clearly working hard. "I know a few sources I could tap."

"Glad we see eye to eye on this." Given their relative positions, he couldn't resist adding, "Literally."

Sam cocked her head. "You might be a fun guy if you lightened up, Mark."

"Did I ever tell you I used to be a stand-up comic?"

That startled her into taking a step backward. "You're kidding!"

"Actually, yes." Score one for his side. "See you later." Striding past, he went up the steps, his senses ablaze from the encounter.

For heaven's sake, they'd been discussing business. She'd only been trying to wheedle support out of him, not get him hot and bothered. Yet, intentionally or not, that's what she'd accomplished.

Mark straightened his tie, which probably didn't need it. Nevertheless, the act reasserted his sense of control as he stepped onto the fifth floor, home to the hospital's main offices. Immediately, he felt his administrator persona settle comfortably over him.

Enough kidding around. He had a job to do, a job he loved.

In the executive suite, his secretary, May Chong, handed Mark a sheaf of phone messages. As he was returning them, the center's public relations director, Jennifer Martin, popped into his office with encouraging statistics about the hospital's toy drive. A few minutes later, staff attorney Tony Franco arrived with a question about a lawsuit. Mark encouraged him to press for arbitration.

He spent most of the morning going over projections for the new fertility center. Although Safe Harbor had remodeled its main building and bragged publicly about its fertility services, it wouldn't achieve world-class status until it recruited a renowned expert to head a showcase program. He or she would bring additional staff and require more lab and office space, so plans were moving rapidly to acquire and renovate the dental building.

Mark felt the adrenaline pulsing through his system. He loved the challenge of pulling together all these different elements and creating something that could enrich people's lives.

Shortly before lunch, May put through a call from

Chandra Yashimoto, vice president of Medical Center Management, Inc., in Louisville. As usual, she wasted no time on small talk. "We have a problem."

A quick mental survey of current issues failed to raise any red flags. "What sort of problem?"

"The owner of the dental building has filed for bankruptcy. We're back to square one on the acquisition."

Damn and double-damn. Yet selling the structure would be in the best interest of the man's creditors. "We're so close to inking a deal. Surely we can come to an understanding."

"You've never dealt with a federal bankruptcy court before, have you? The whole thing could drag on for years." Chandra released an impatient breath. "We have to look elsewhere."

No sense debating the point; they needed to move forward with all due speed. "I'll start researching other buildings on the market." They ought to be able to find something within a ten-to-fifteen-minute drive. Safe Harbor was part of bustling Orange County, with a population of more than three million.

"That will throw us months behind schedule." The veep went on to say that a delay would cost a fortune in lost revenue. She was determined to hire a director and get the new center operational as quickly as possible. "We've decided to use facilities we already own. For starters, we'll be taking over that office suite on your floor, the one where you put the memorial—whatchamacallit—counseling clinic."

Sam's center? Well, it didn't *have* to be next to the administrative suite. "We could move it next door to the medical building. I believe there are a couple of vacant offices."

"Our new director and his or her colleagues will need those. That's valuable space, Mark."

He reviewed his rapidly dwindling options. "We have an empty storage area in the basement that can be fixed up." Sam would simply have to make the best of the situation.

"I've earmarked that space for an embryology lab," Chandra said. "The clinic's going to have to find other quarters. *Away* from the hospital."

Mark barely stifled a groan. This could mean the end of Sam's dream. Perhaps not immediately; she might find space at some other facility in town. But the clinic's association with the hospital gave it prestige and prominence. Without those, she was unlikely to attract more than subsistence-level funding.

"And, Mark?" Chandra's voice roused him from his grim reflections.

"Yes?" he asked warily.

"Put a muzzle on that pediatrician, will you? We can't have her blowing this thing out of proportion."

"I'll do my best." As if you could muzzle Dr. Samantha Forrest.

After he hung up, Mark leaned back and stared at the ceiling. The acoustical tile offered neither inspiration nor reassurance.

Instead, he kept seeing Sam holding her fiesta in the parking lot, proclaiming to the press that Scrooge and the Grinch had merged into the shape of Mark Rayburn, M.D.

No wonder he hated Christmas.

Chapter Two

Before heading for her office next door, Sam paid a visit to the hospital's intermediate-care nursery. Adorable in their tiny caps and booties, the triplets lay in side-by-side bassinets. The low-level lights and quiet environment were designed to reduce stress for the infants, but to grown-ups like her, simply gazing at little Connie, Courtney and Colin was enough to lower her blood pressure.

Sam loved those perfect little fingers and hands. Even the wrinkly, pouchy appearance that distinguished newborns filled her with delight. She found herself humming an old lullaby. "Where are you going, my little one, little one…"

Okay, enough self-indulgence. Time to get moving.

Despite her resolve, she spent much of the morning thinking about kids. That was understandable, considering that her hours were spent peering into small ears, discussing immunization schedules with concerned parents, answering questions about breastfeeding, evaluating rashes, assessing infant development and writing a couple of referrals to specialists.

But she wasn't only thinking about other people's kids. She was thinking about her own—or, rather, the fact that she was thirty-six and hadn't had any yet.

These past few weeks, the combination of holiday

celebrations and her annual physical had reminded her of how quickly life was racing by. With current technology, she still had another five years or so to bear children. But there was the not-so-small matter of deciding whether to go it alone or put more effort into finding a husband.

She'd had a couple of serious relationships, both with men she'd met through her activities in championing children's causes. Shared zeal made for hot sex—Samantha could attest to that. Ultimately, though, either the passion had cooled along with the cause, or she'd come to realize the guy was drawn to her energy and purpose because he lacked sufficient of his own. She needed a man strong enough to stand beside her as an equal.

On the other hand, not one so bullheaded he was always blocking her path. An image of Mark on the stairway this morning kept appearing on her mental screen. Since the hospital's new owner hired him as administrator, he'd become Public Enemy Number One as far as she was concerned.

Then, a few weeks ago, she'd stopped into the nursery to admire Tony Franco's baby, and spotted Mark cradling the newborn in his arms. His face illuminated with tenderness, he'd cooed to the little girl as if she were his own daughter. Sam had slipped away, oddly moved.

Why didn't Mark have a wife and children? How unfair that men could ignore the biological clock that ticked so loudly for women.

Well, no point in woolgathering, Samantha thought as she washed up following her last patient of the morning. She had a busy afternoon ahead, dealing with departmental paperwork and formulating plans for the Christmas fundraiser. She felt certain she could count on the support of the PR director, since the clinic was named for the baby son that Jennifer Serra—Jennifer Martin, since her recent marriage—had lost during a troubled teen pregnancy.

Sam decided to see if she could catch Jennifer for a quick brainstorming session. As she ducked into the hall, however, her nurse called from behind, "Don't forget!"

"Don't forget what?" Sam swung back toward the ever-efficient Devina Gupta.

"Dr. Kendall wants to see you," said the nurse, a bronze-skinned woman who looked too young to have a son in medical school. "I've told you three times."

Oh, bother. The gynecologist had run tests during Sam's checkup and insisted on discussing the results in person. In Sam's opinion, becoming a doctor ought to excuse you from undergoing medical tests. It should make you immune to all illnesses, too.

But of course it didn't.

"I'll stop by her office," Sam promised, checking her watch. Nora Kendall's office was located one floor below. If she dawdled a few more minutes, she should be safe because Nora would probably leave for lunch.

"I'll call to let her know you're coming," Devina said. "I'm sure she'll wait."

Even the stubbornest person couldn't win every time. "Thank you."

"Not a problem. Better hurry!"

Reluctantly, Samantha obeyed her nurse.

PASTRAMI HEAPED ON RYE. Did a pickle count as a vegetable? And mustard. That had a few nutrients, right?

Mark relished his meal at a corner table in the hospital cafeteria while skimming the latest medical journal. He also kept an eye open for Samantha. Not that he would break the devastating news to her in public, but he hoped to track her movements and catch her on the way back to her office. With luck, he might find an isolated setting where her outraged screams wouldn't attract too much notice.

She often ate with Lori and Jennifer, who were talking earnestly over their chicken-à-la-something. Judging by Lori's quivering mouth, the subject must be Dr. Sellers.

The cause of their breakup was no secret. As the eldest of six girls, Lori had spent her teen years serving as second mother to five argumentative siblings. She'd sworn off having kids, and her fiancé, who'd recently completed an exhausting residency, had agreed he wanted to spend his free time relaxing with the woman he loved, just the two of them.

Then he'd changed his mind. Mark wasn't sure why, but since the neonatologist spent most of his time around babies, no doubt he'd eventually come to embrace these magnificent little people, so filled with promise and love and…

Am I talking about Jared or about myself?

Mark loved babies and kids of all ages. Delightful images of youngsters he'd delivered filled a folder in his computer. He'd even had a few named after him.

But fathering one? Not a good plan. While he'd escaped his family's weakness for substance abuse, he had no desire to risk passing it on to another generation. Especially since he'd learned the hard way that there were some battles you couldn't win, no matter how much you loved a person.

Besides, he had no time for children of his own. His baby was the new fertility center.

In front of him, the magazine drifted shut. Just as well, since he hadn't read a word.

Mark chewed the last bite of his sandwich. Amazingly, no one had interrupted his meal with an emergency or even so much as a question. That had to be a first.

A glance showed Jennifer and Lori still conferring

without their third musketeer. Perhaps Sam was still with patients, or she'd decided to run errands instead of eating. But, he couldn't afford to put this off. News of the dental building's involvement in a bankruptcy had already reached Tony, who'd come in to make sure Mark had received word. Sam needed to be prepared.

Mark cleared his dishes and set out for the building next door.

"I DON'T SUPPOSE IT HELPS to point out that things could be worse," Nora Kendall told Sam ruefully. They were sitting in Nora's office, beneath photos of babies and framed diplomas proclaiming her expertise in obstetrics, gynecology and fertility.

Fertility. The word cut like a scalpel.

"I know I'm lucky to still be cancer-free after twenty years," Sam conceded. "But... Are you certain it's early menopause?"

"Would you like me to go over the results again?"

Sam waved away the offer. Despite her question, she understood the test results all too well. She'd known this was possible; she simply hadn't believed it would happen to her.

Girls who survived cancer treatment as teens were more than a dozen times as likely as other women to suffer menopause before age forty. The greatest risk was for those who, like Sam, had received heavy doses of radiation and chemotherapy to battle Hodgkin's lymphoma. The damage to the ovaries couldn't be repaired.

"What about fertility treatments?" With no husband on the horizon, that would mean using donor sperm. Not Sam's preference, but if it was her only chance to conceive...

Compassion shaded Nora's expression. "At this stage,

you'd require donated eggs and heavy-duty hormone treatment. In view of your medical history, I don't recommend it," she added gently.

The instinct to fight swelled in Sam. It was the same instinct that had saved her as a teenager and by which she'd lived ever since. But she had to be reasonable. "You think trying to have a baby might harm my health?"

"That is definitely a concern."

"I don't want to be an idiot about this," she conceded. *And I know the dangers as well as anyone.*

Nora showed no impatience, although she must be hungry. "This is a heavy blow to absorb. If you strongly want to try for a baby, I'll do my best to help you."

Sam tossed back her head. Despite her dejected mood, she relished the bounce of long hair, which she never took for granted. Years ago, she'd put on a brave face about baldness and colorful scarves, but in reality she'd hated them.

"No, thanks. You're right, it could be worse. These past few months, when I started getting irregular periods and night sweats, I was afraid the cancer had returned." Night sweats and swollen glands were the symptoms that had first alerted her to the lymphoma. "I'm darn lucky."

"You pooh-poohed the idea of a recurrence during the exam," Nora pointed out.

"I'd hate to act like a crybaby," Sam explained. "Besides, it's counterproductive to dwell on things we can't control."

"Counterproductive but natural," her doctor responded. "Don't feel you have to hold everything inside and put on a brave face for my sake. Sometimes it's healthy to cry."

"Not for me, it isn't." Because her voice sounded shaky, Sam rose quickly. "I've kept you long enough. Go eat."

"I don't mind skipping lunch," Nora said.

"It's hard to be good-natured with patients when you're hungry." Sam had learned that from experience. "Speaking of eating, you're invited to an open house at the counseling clinic on Christmas Day."

"Christmas? Gee, I'd love to come, but I promised to fix the turkey for my aunt's dinner."

Oh, dear. Perhaps because her family lived far away, Sam had blithely figured most of her friends, at least the unmarried ones, would be available. But she just couldn't focus on that now.

"We'll miss you. Well, thanks for everything." Sam grabbed her purse and bolted for the door. If she lingered one more second, she might break down.

Outside on the walkway, she dragged in a series of deep breaths, trying to ease the sensation of having been punched in the stomach. She would never feel a baby move inside her. Never have any funny-awful pregnancy stories to share with her patients. Never experience the wonder of breastfeeding.

Every day, she cuddled infants and went nose to nose with inquisitive toddlers. For their parents and for teen mothers like Candy, she served as the sage counselor. Sam felt like a sailor lost at sea, dying of thirst while floating on an ocean of undrinkable water.

She wished her parents were here, and her brother, Benton, a cardiologist who lived in her hometown of Seattle with his wife and two kids. They'd rallied behind her before, and they'd do it now. Benton had urged her more than once to relocate to his area, where she had a lot of old friends. The last time she'd visited her parents' clinic in Mexico, she'd also given serious consideration to moving there to work with children in need.

Yet for once she didn't feel like turning to her family. How could they understand? Mom had conceived and given birth easily, and Benton and his wife had produced their kids on a prearranged schedule. *First a boy, then a girl, two and a half years apart.*

Self-pity was not her style, Samantha reminded herself. Neither was resenting other people's good fortune. What she ought to do was square her shoulders, lift her chin and go comfort Lori about *her* problems.

"Oh, there you are." The baritone voice gave her a start.

Mark Rayburn shouldn't sneak up on people. Well, with a delivery truck rumbling across the quadrangle and a medical rescue copter whirring toward the hospital's helipad, perhaps he hadn't actually needed to sneak.

"Samantha?" he prodded, looking much too solid and comforting for her fragile peace of mind. "Are you all right?"

She tried to shrug and look nonchalant. Useless.

"No," she gasped. "No, Mark, I'm not all right."

Then, to her utter humiliation, she burst into tears.

IN THE TWO YEARS MARK HAD worked with the fiery Samantha Forrest, he'd never before glimpsed this lost, little-girl expression. Impulsively, he gathered her into his arms. Felt her collapse against his chest, registered the trace of tears against his neck and tried to soothe the shudders wracking her body. It hurt to see her in such pain.

"What's wrong?" he asked.

The Sam he knew would have volleyed back a sharp answer. Today, she simply went on pouring out grief as if she'd bottled it up for years.

Around them, the medical complex lay calm. During the noon hour, no patients were arriving to notice her distress, and the noise of the helicopter covered her sobs. But any moment that would change, and he suspected Sam would be embarrassed if others witnessed her in this state.

They ought to go somewhere private, as long as that didn't require navigating a hallway or passing a receptionist. Much as Mark loved this place and its people, he deplored the pervasive gossip.

"Let's take a walk," he suggested.

Sam gave a faint nod. She clung to his arm unsteadily as he guided her between the buildings and through a landscaped park strip.

He wondered again what had upset her so badly. It couldn't be related to the counseling clinic, because if she'd learned about that, she'd have railed at him rather than fallen apart. The loss of a patient? That certainly could be upsetting. Still, he'd never seen her react at such a personal level.

They crossed the pedestrian bridge over Coast Highway and reached the edge of the bluffs, where a long wooden staircase led down to the beach. A salty breeze stung Mark's cheeks as they descended and, beside him, Sam sucked in a couple of deep breaths.

"Is your family okay?" he asked as they crossed the beach parking area, largely deserted on a December weekday.

"As far as I know." She sounded puzzled.

"You don't have to talk if you don't want to," Mark said.

Sam peered across the sand toward the soothing lap of the surf. "What're we doing here?"

"Taking a break. Hey, are you lost in a daze?"

"I guess so."

This was unlike her. It worried him.

They found rocky perches on adjacent boulders that bordered the sand. Overhead, a seagull wheeled, mewing plaintively. Aside from a few hardy surfers plying their boards on the low waves, they were alone.

"I figured we could both use a breather," Mark added.

"Thanks."

"You're welcome." The fact that he had a bomb to drop on her bothered him more than a little. But in view of her distress, the clinic's situation could wait.

Samantha managed a weak smile. "You must think I've lost my mind."

He seized on the opening to ask, "What happened?"

She leaned back on the rock, tilting her lightly tanned face toward the winter sun. "You remind me of a doctor on an old TV show. A kind, wise fellow everyone came to for advice."

"Hardly anyone comes to me for advice," Mark said wryly. "And if I give it to them, they don't follow it."

Samantha chuckled. "The heck they don't."

"Well, my patients might be the exception."

"And the staff."

"Not very often."

She fell silent, as if debating how far to trust him. After a moment, she broke the lull. "I got bad news from my doctor."

Clouds drifted over the sun, casting the beach into gray gloom. A chill ran through Mark. Since taking the helm at Safe Harbor, he'd worked his way through the personnel files of his medical staff, acquainting himself with their backgrounds. While they weren't required to disclose their personal medical histories, Samantha had done so freely.

He loosened his tie because he was having a hard time swallowing past the lump in his throat. "The cancer's returned?"

Her startled gaze met his. "No. No, that's not it, thank goodness."

What a relief. "I'm glad to hear it." Very glad.

He waited, in case she had more to say. Out on the water, a surfer rode a puny wave to shore, then stepped off the board with a disdainful grimace. "Pathetic waves," Mark muttered in sympathy.

"I beg your pardon?"

"The surf. It's feeble."

"What're you, a surfing critic?" she demanded.

"I used to surf in high school," he said. "They have surf in Miami, you know."

"I thought you played football."

"The two sports aren't mutually exclusive."

"I never said they were." Samantha kicked at the sand.

The spray hit Mark's freshly shined shoes and sifted into his socks. "Thank you for that."

"My pleasure." She started to laugh. Almost in slow motion, her face crumpled. Finally she rasped out, "It's early menopause."

So that was the bad news. "Because of the radiation and chemo?"

She nodded. "Nora advises against fertility treatments. She says they'd be hazardous."

"I concur," Mark said.

Fresh tears tracked after the ones that had dried in the breeze. "I didn't realize how much I counted on having children. On going through the whole experience of pregnancy."

He checked the impulse to point out that she could adopt. You didn't console a woman who'd lost a child by telling her she could have more, and, in a sense, that's what had happened to Samantha. He'd learned from his patients that the child in a woman's dreams might seem almost as real to her as a baby she'd held in her arms.

How ironic that, despite his medical expertise, he had nothing to offer. Except comfort.

Mark moved to her rock and slid his arm around her. When Sam's head drifted to his shoulder, he brushed a kiss across her hair.

She nestled closer, the scent of springtime enveloping him for a sweet instant before the breeze whipped it away. He couldn't resist tracing the delicate straightness of her nose with his lips, and when she blinked up at him, his mouth closed instinctively over hers.

The warmth drew him in, tantalizing against the cool air. This might be crazy, but Mark yielded to the longing to pull her onto his lap. She shifted readily, clinging to him, answering his kisses with a flick of tongue and a soft moan.

He felt himself stirring, coming alive, wanting Sam in a way he'd never allowed himself before. He lifted his head, breathing fast, and then touched his forehead to hers.

Although he wasn't sure about the wisdom of proceeding with such a combustible relationship, they could hardly deny their attraction. And they were both adults. "We should get together after work. Figure out where to go from here."

"Where to go?" Sam drew back, a pucker forming between her eyebrows.

"I didn't mean literally. I meant…" Grim reality slapped Mark, along with a fresh blast of wind. How could he have forgotten about Chandra's call? "Wait. Before we discuss anything personal, I have a piece of news."

"Hit me with it," Sam replied, sounding more like her usual tart self. "Maybe that'll bring us both to our senses."

Unfortunately, he reflected, it was more likely to bring them to the point of open warfare. "It's about the clinic..."

Chapter Three

Samantha couldn't believe what she was hearing. Yet despite her dismay, she felt conflicted and uncertain. Where was the instantaneous flare of anger that should have powered her into action?

She'd worked hard to bring this counseling service to reality. While she admired her parents' devotion to the poor of another country, there were people hurting in this affluent area, too. Women in abusive relationships who needed someone to talk to, as well as confused teenagers and former foster children who lacked survival skills. They couldn't afford to pay and often shrank from paperwork and bureaucracies.

The Serra Clinic was unusually informal and flexible, using peer counselors who empathized with their clients. Right now, it depended entirely on volunteers, but Sam had hoped to raise funds and find sponsors so they could hire a professional staff, as well. Now, the entire project might be wiped out, or reduced to a catch-as-catch-can enterprise that limped along in second-rate facilities.

She ought to be furious with Mark, who she knew sided with the corporation. Instead, she kept wishing this awful displacement had waited a few more weeks or months so she could go on enjoying the comfort of his arms.

What was wrong with her?

You've received two severe blows in the space of an afternoon. No wonder you're reeling.

Ah, that was the Dr. Forrest side of her brain kicking in. But reeling or not, it didn't explain the way she'd reacted to Mark.

She'd felt a strong urge to skip out on their duties and do much more than kiss him. To pull off his tie, and his jacket, and the rest of his clothes—not in public of course, but...

"Sam? I understand why you're distracted but I'm getting a little worried." The subject of her fantasy stopped pacing along the sand and regarded her with dark-eyed tenderness.

Sam wriggled as the rock dug into her bottom. "Because I'm not erupting like a volcano?"

"That would be a more typical reaction, yes."

"I can't believe they're doing this to people in need. It's cruel."

"It's business," Mark replied. "The hospital has a core mission, and your project isn't part of it."

"That's where we disagree—in spades." There it was, a trace of irritation. Sam did her best to fan it into full-blown righteous anger. "You have to see how important counseling is."

"Yes, of course, but—"

"Keep on compromising your values, and one day you won't have a soul left to call your own."

"Oh, **really?**" he countered. "You should try compromising more often. You might actually accomplish something instead of spinning your wheels."

"That's what you think I'm doing? Spinning my wheels?"

"Go ahead and pick an argument." He seemed almost pleased. "I prefer that to seeing you defeated. Go on, Sam. Call me names if it makes you happy."

Did he have to look so rumpled and obliging? Mark Rayburn, guiding spirit of the medical center, everyone's favorite go-to guy. *The enemy.* Yet she still failed to summon any significant fury.

"This is not one of my favorite days," Sam muttered. "I wish I'd checked my horoscope before I got out of bed this morning."

His chuckle reverberated. "I doubt that would have helped. But take the afternoon off. You've got a lot to think about."

"I never take the afternoon off."

"What were you planning to do that's so important?"

She tried to remember. Paperwork. The Christmas fundraiser. Oh, heavens. Was she even going to have a place to hold it? "How soon are they kicking us out?"

"We didn't discuss a deadline," Mark said. "I'm sure I can hold off until after the first of the year, if you like."

"Yes. For one thing, I need to break this to our volunteers." And find somewhere to stow the computers and furniture they'd acquired. Samantha's brain whirred. "I guess I will go home for an hour or so. I can think better uninterrupted."

They recrossed the footbridge in silence. Every now and then, a flicker of indignation crossed her mental horizon—did he have to break the news to her when she was already down and out?—but she had to acknowledge that delaying wouldn't have made things easier.

Sam hated seeing the issue from Mark's perspective. It made her so grumpy, she barely mumbled a farewell when they reached the edge of the hospital complex, and strode off without a backward glance. Nevertheless, she sensed the moment when he stopped watching her and turned onto his own path.

She stemmed an impulse to call out. What would she say, anyway? *Next time I see you, I'll bring poison darts.*

How strange it felt, walking home in the middle of the day when she ought to be at the hospital. She'd scarcely taken a day off since entering medical school. Even in the summers, she'd worked hard to pay the tuition. Putting two kids through medical school had been expensive for her parents, who'd spent most of their careers doing low-paid work among the poor.

Sam had vowed to continue their tradition, and hadn't entirely written off the idea of someday joining their clinic. But with student loans to pay, she'd had to accept a mainstream medical position and consign charity work to her free hours. Although she'd recently paid off the last of the loans, she still needed to build up at least a modest savings account.

There was, fortunately, an inheritance from her grandparents that she'd invested and saved as an emergency fund. Her parents had refused to let her touch it when she was younger, saying she should only draw on it if she absolutely had to.

She'd always figured the fund was there for the children she planned to have one day. If there'd been any reasonable chance that fertility treatments would work without destroying her health, she'd have spent the money without question now.

It might enable her to adopt. The prospect of a long search and the complex procedures involved seemed overwhelming in her present state of mind, but at least, when she was ready, she had the money set aside.

Silently, she thanked her grandparents. And missed them.

Rounding a corner, Sam had to make way for two women chatting as they pushed strollers side by side along the sidewalk. Their babies, one in a darling miniature ski jacket and the other merry in a green-and-red plaid coat, leaned eagerly forward as if trying to embrace the world.

Feeling a sudden ache, Sam averted her gaze, only to find herself peering through a house window at a Christmas tree surrounded by gaily wrapped toys. Everywhere she looked, there seemed to be children and families.

A lump rose in her throat. She'd always assumed she would eventually have those things, too. And maybe she could, but not the way she'd expected.

To focus on her loss felt selfish in view of the clinic's crisis and her own fundamental good health. *Be grateful you aren't facing death.*

The problem was, now she had to face life.

ON FRIDAY AFTERNOON, MARK SAT in front of his computer, fingering the mouse as he sifted through applications for the position of fertility center director. Medical Center Management had asked him to narrow the field to three top candidates. Not an easy task. Among several dozen applicants, at least six offered excellent credentials. Not brilliant, perhaps, but close.

Leaning back, he tented his fingers and glanced through the window toward the harbor. Somehow the water managed to sparkle even in the weak winter sunlight.

Was it really only two days since he'd sat on the beach with Samantha? Felt like aeons.

Flexing his hands, he wondered at this nagging concern and the sense that he ought to do something for her. Yesterday, he'd sought a moment to talk to Sam after a staff meeting, but she'd hurried off to admit a patient. He wasn't sure what he'd have said, anyway. He had no magic wand to rescue the counseling clinic nor, despite all his training, could he remedy her medical condition.

Their kiss hadn't softened her attitude toward him. Still the same cautious distance. The same awareness that they stood, irrevocably, on opposite sides of a battlefield.

It had affected *him*, though. He missed her. Those sparks, that sudden burst of passion—his body heated at the memory.

You must have a death wish, Rayburn.

Mark returned his attention to the résumé on the screen. How ironic that all these fertility experts had no cure for early menopause, either.

Still, the woman whose credentials lay before him had an impressive background at Johns Hopkins and Yale. She specialized in genetic engineering that could enable parents to deliver healthy babies free of their families' devastating hereditary conditions. Her cover letter indicated she was interested in moving to southern California to be closer to her elderly parents.

Much as he admired her, Mark knew she'd be a better fit at a research-oriented university hospital. Safe Harbor needed a clinician concerned with applying proven techniques as well as developing and testing new ones.

The prospect of having the best possible staff and lab facilities thrilled him. He wasn't entirely sorry about taking over existing space at Safe Harbor, because it meant that the new center would be up and running much faster than under the old plan. But he had to find the right director, and so far, respectable as these applicants were, none quite fit what he envisioned.

May Chong buzzed him on the intercom. "There's a woman on line three who says she's your sister. Do you want to pick up?"

A jolt of relief drove everything else from Mark's mind. "Absolutely." Then a wave of apprehension closed over him. It had been five years since he'd seen her. What kind of condition was she in? Would she even be coherent? Was she calling from a jail, seeking bail money?

He punched the button and asked cautiously, "Bryn?"

"You moved," she said without preamble. "I pictured you still in Florida."

"I'd have left a forwarding address if I'd known where to send it."

"I found you on the internet."

Her voice had a huskier quality than he remembered. The last time they'd met he'd seen the toll that drugs and alcohol had taken on his sister, sprinkling her brown hair with premature traces of gray and leaving pouches beneath her eyes.

"You're easy to find," she added. "Unlike me, I guess."

"I hired a detective, but you dropped completely out of sight. Are you okay? Where are you?" He braced for her usual evasions.

"In Phoenix. I've been clean for two years."

"Two years? Congratulations." That sounded like an eternity, considering that she'd begun using as a teenager and hadn't stopped except for the few times he'd persuaded her to enter rehab programs. She must be thirty-three now. Hard to imagine his baby sister being that old. "I wish you'd let me know sooner."

"I wanted to be sure I could do this on my own." In the background, he heard the rumble of a large engine.

"Are you at a truck stop?" That would be typical, sad to say. According to the detective, his sister had put her health and life at risk, picking up men for drug money.

"I work as a receptionist for a trucking company," she told him. "Mark, I don't blame you for doubting me. I put you through hell. But I've found a group that supports me. It's called Celebrate Recovery—kind of like Alcoholics Anonymous, only it's at a church."

"I'm glad to hear it." Beneath her casual tone, he sensed that she'd called for a reason. "I'm happier than I can say to learn that you're all right. You're the only family I have."

"No wife?" Bryn asked. "I was hoping for a few nieces and nephews by now."

"Not yet. I'm still marveling at the idea that a home can be a refuge instead of a war zone." Now, where had that come from?

"So you choose to be alone?"

"I'm not alone. I run a hospital and see patients. Long hours, but it's what I always dreamed of." Enough talking about himself. He wanted to find out more about his sister. "I was going to ask—"

"Why I'm calling," she finished. "Because I always call with a motive, right?"

"That is the pattern, yes." Blinking buttons on the phone caught Mark's attention. People must be trying to reach him. Thank goodness his secretary had the sense to deflect them.

"One of the steps in our recovery is making amends to people we've harmed. And you're the person I've hurt the most."

"You want to make amends?" He didn't see how a

person could atone for so many years of disappointment and pain. Still, he loved her in spite of that.

"Maybe not for your sake, but for mine—if that's okay?" Bryn added quickly. "The last thing I want is to cause you any more problems."

Forgiveness might not come easily, but Mark was willing to try. "I'd be happy to see you."

"I was hoping…how about Christmas?" she blurted. "I could drive out there."

"That's what, seven or eight hours?" A long trek for one person. "I'll send you a plane ticket."

"No, Mark. This is my responsibility." She spoke with a maturity he'd never heard from her before. "I should arrive by late afternoon. But don't let me disrupt your plans if you were going to spend Christmas with someone."

That reminded him of Sam's fundraiser. He'd promised to be there, but that didn't preclude welcoming his sister. "You should come," Mark told her. "It won't be a proper Christmas without you."

"I don't deserve…" Her words choked off. She cleared her throat. "You're the most wonderful brother in the world."

"Just get here in one piece." He gave her his cell phone number. "You can reach me anytime."

She provided her own number. "I'm not going to disappear again. This is for keeps."

"That's the best Christmas present you could give me."

After they hung up, Mark sat amazed at this development. He'd feared his next contact with Bryn would be a call informing him of her death, or that he might never learn what happened to her. This was beyond anything he'd dared to hope for.

If it was real, and not just another of her deceptions.

A tap at the door broke his reverie. Without waiting for an invitation, a blond whirlwind in a teal blouse and gray tweed skirt breezed in, head high and mouth set in a determined line.

"Sam." Mark got to his feet. "I was wondering where you've been."

"Licking my wounds. Well, I'm done with the self-pity. Now I've got a plan."

"What kind of plan?" he asked warily.

"I've decided to call a press conference."

"Excuse me?"

She beamed. "I'm sure reporters will be very interested to know what's happening to the clinic."

"I decide when the hospital holds a press conference and what information we release to the media."

She held up her hands in a peace gesture. "Sorry. I was just taking a poke at you. I want to announce the Christmas fundraiser. That's all."

"Why not simply send out a press release?" Putting Samantha together with the media was like cleaning a linoleum floor with gasoline. One spark and the whole house blew up.

"It'll get lost on somebody's desk. There's only a couple of weeks left, after all, and this is the fastest way to reach our supporters. Also, a local caterer agreed to provide food at cost in return for publicity. Jennifer believes we can get the press conference organized by Monday." With an unexpected note of pleading, Sam added, "Please? If the fundraiser fizzles, we're sunk."

It was hard to argue when she spoke so reasonably. "I suppose so. No mention of having to move out of the offices, though," Mark warned. "We'll be presenting the plans for the fertility center in a controlled manner. I can't have you hijacking the subject."

"And flying it into the side of a mountain?" Samantha observed wryly.

"Do I have to remind you about past slipups? Such as the time you announced on the internet that we were giving away beauty makeovers?" Mark would never forget the uproar when a swarm of Samantha's teen moms—including Candy—arrived at the hospital to demand free pampering.

"I just said we ought to make single moms who keep their babies feel like Cinderellas at the ball, even if it meant providing..." She shook her head. "That was over the top, I admit. But it turned out all right." A local salon, glad to reap the TV coverage, had donated makeovers.

"This is much more serious. Bad publicity about the hospital could hurt our recruitment efforts and shake up stockholder confidence." And he'd lose the chance to re-cruit the kind of director who could put Safe Harbor on the map.

"You don't need to lecture me, Mark."

They faced each other across his desk, a gulf that seemed wider than ever. He wished he knew how to cross it, not just for the sake of their professional relationship, but because he had a very strong desire to kiss her again. Right now. No matter who might walk in on them.

With a mental wrench, he returned to the topic. "What time Monday?"

"One o'clock."

"We'll go over the presentation beforehand. You, me and Jennifer."

"You plan to be there?"

He shrugged. "I'll put it an appearance."

Sam folded her arms. "If you insist. But honestly, boss, I promise to color inside the lines."

"Spoken like a pediatrician."

When she grinned, sunshine flooded the office. "We really are on the same team, most of the time."

After she left, Mark took a moment to remember how to breathe. Then he got back to work.

Chapter Four

Through the window of the Sea Star Café, the gray sky gave the harbor a flat, subdued air. Once darkness fell tonight, strings of holiday lights on the moored sailboats and yachts would provide a fairyland display, but this morning the scene matched Samantha's gloomy mood.

Lori slid into a seat beside her at the table, the aroma of spices wafting from her steaming cup of chai. Joining them, Jennifer set down a mug of coffee. Their faint reflections in the window showed the contrast between Sam's own blond ponytail, Lori's reddish-brown hair and Jennifer's darker coloring, a tribute to a Hispanic heritage on her father's side.

That reminded Sam: she'd always wondered what *her* children would look like. Well, she wasn't going to have any. Not genetic ones, anyway.

"If you stare out the window any harder, the glass is going to shatter," Lori said.

"Or you'll focus the light and set fire to one of the sailboats," Jennifer added.

"I'm entitled to be moody," Sam grumped. "Deal with it."

She'd broken the news about her medical results to her friends yesterday, and had hoped they could all put the subject behind them before their regular Saturday power walk and coffee-guzzling. Instead, Sam sat here brooding. Well, they ought to understand.

"We *are* dealing with it, by making jokes," said Lori.

"At your expense." Jennifer softened her words with a smile. "In the nicest way possible." With an adopted three-month-old and an adoring husband, the newlywed beamed at everyone and everything. Constantly. To the verge of being nauseating.

Honestly, how could she sink so low as to resent her friend? Sam thought in dismay. Just because she was suffering herself didn't mean she wished the same misery on anyone else.

She looked up to see Lori frowning. "Sam, I never thought you were that eager to have kids. You always seemed preoccupied with saving the world."

True enough. "Frankly, my reaction surprises me, too. I should be worrying about the counseling clinic, not my silly personal issues."

"Early menopause is hardly a silly personal issue," Jennifer said.

"Well, it *is* personal. But it's not silly." Lori eyed a cinnamon-nut muffin passing by on someone's plate. "You think I worked off enough calories to eat one of those? I'd hate to lose my girlish figure, especially now that I'm single again." Perhaps realizing that she hadn't actually been married, she added, "In the totally unattached sense."

"Do you feel ready to date?" Jennifer asked. "That would be a good sign."

Lori shrugged. "Wish I did. Then I might stop obsessing about Jared. Only...every guy I meet, when he finds out I'm an obstetrical nurse, the first thing he says is how much he wants kids. Can you believe it?"

"Yes." To her embarrassment, Samantha felt the sting of tears. What was wrong with her?

"I'm sorry. I keep forgetting you can't *have*..." Lori grimaced. "That's even worse, me *dwelling* on it."

"We should find a neutral topic. Unless you two would rather discuss your...issues." Jennifer peered from one to the other. "It's fine with me either way."

"Do you have to be so *nice?*" Sam roared.

Lori held up her hands. "I've got an idea. Let's talk about somebody we all hate."

"I don't hate anyone," Jennifer said.

"Mark," Sam proposed.

Lori shook her head. "It's not his fault he's booting out the counseling clinic. Besides, I can't hate him. He's my doctor."

"Neither can I. After all, he hired me," Jennifer reminded them. "And he's a great boss."

Sam didn't hate him, either. The truth was, she'd done far too much thinking about Mark during the past few days. Did he guess how she melted inside when he drew close? A part of her wished they'd followed up on his suggestion to figure out how to proceed after their kiss. If only the stupid hospital corporation hadn't thrown a wrench into everything.

If only I weren't wildly attracted to the wrong man.

"Why *do* you hate Mark?" Jennifer asked. "Seriously, I realize you two cross swords on a regular basis, but I figured there were sparks."

Was it that obvious?

"He may drive you crazy, but he's supportive when you need him," Lori declared.

That did it. "Let me tell you about men," Sam burst out. "First they're all warm and supportive, but the next thing you know they sucker you into darning their socks."

"Dr. Rayburn would never ask anyone to darn his socks." Lori stirred her tea so vigorously it slopped over. "When they get a hole in them, he throws them away and buys new ones." Amazing what details some nurses noticed about their physicians.

"Who asked you to darn his socks?" Jennifer asked.

"Well, no one, literally," Samantha admitted. "But there was this guy I almost married in college. I nearly dropped my plans for med school so I could put *him* through law school." Brad Worthy. Or rather, Brad *Un*Worthy. She saw his high-boned, angular face as clearly as if she'd dated him last month instead of fifteen years ago at UC Berkeley.

"He must have been an exciting guy, if you cared that much about him," Lori said.

"Smart and passionate." And terribly hurt when his starry-eyed girlfriend came to her senses. "He couldn't figure out why I put my dreams ahead of his."

"Why couldn't you both pursue your dreams?" Jennifer asked.

"Too expensive. Well, from his perspective." Brad had freaked out at the prospect of running up hundreds of thousands of dollars in debt between them. "I didn't care if we ever owned a house or sent our kids to private school. But he did."

"He broke up with you over that?" Lori said. "He sounds like a snob."

"Lucky you discovered that you had such different values," Jennifer added.

In retrospect, their breakup *had* been lucky, Sam reflected as she checked her watch. "I'm afraid I have to go. Candy's being released this morning. I want to make sure she and the triplets are okay."

Lori regarded her dubiously. "It's after ten. She might have left already."

With a guilty pang, Sam realized she'd been dragging her feet. These past few days, seeing those three darling babies had reminded her painfully of her own condition, and she'd found it increasingly hard to sympathize with the serious challenges Candy faced.

First you resent your friends, and now you envy a young mother you've mentored? What's wrong with you?

Sam hauled herself to her feet. "Please forgive my bad mood this morning."

"I will, if you'll forgive *me* for boring you to death about my broken heart," said Lori.

"And if you'll excuse me showing you my honeymoon pictures twice by mistake," Jennifer put in.

"They're great pictures. I didn't mind a bit." Scooping up her oversize purse, Samantha said goodbye and emerged from the cozy café into the chilly seaside air.

She set out at a brisk pace on the uphill march to the hospital. A couple of cyclists swooped by, muscular legs pumping as they bent low over their racing bikes. From a nearby veterinary kennel, a chorus of barks welcomed a visitor or perhaps a meal.

Sam kept an eye out for an empty storefront or sign advertising a small office that might house the counseling clinic. A place right along busy Safe Harbor Boulevard would at least draw walk-in traffic. But how was she going to pay the rent? The hospital facilities had been free.

Somehow, today, she couldn't spare any more energy for other people, even those who were suffering. She just wanted to move past her own deep pain. Thank goodness for exercise.

A few minutes later, her leg muscles burning, she strode into the medical center elevator. On the third floor, the

doors opened on three volunteers wheeling a trio of bassinets toward her, trailed by Candy in the obligatory wheelchair. Sam's heart lurched when she spotted sweet little
Connie with her strawberry blotch.

I'm going to miss her.

"Hey, Doc!" Toward her ambled the father, Jon, a thin
fellow with scraggly facial hair. "Where've you been?"

"I came to the hospital earlier to examine them." She'd
cleared each of the babies for release before leaving to meet
her friends. "Congratulations. Your children are in great
condition. That's not always the case in multiple births."

"I thought you were going to fix her." He indicated
Connie.

Like a broken toy? "We'll deal with the birthmark when
she's older and stronger." Although the triplets had arrived in remarkably good shape, Samantha preferred to
let the infant gain weight before subjecting her to laser
treatment.

The wheelchair rolled alongside them, its occupant
frowning. "This is kind of scary. I'm not sure how I'm
going to care for all these babies when it takes three volunteers just to push the bassinets."

Candy did face a daunting task. Sam had spent a lot of
time reviewing the issues with her in advance, and despite
the occasional hesitation, the girl had seemed determined.
*But was she responding to my enthusiasm? Did I influence
her too much?*

This was hardly the moment for a change of heart.
Once Candy settled in, with help from her mother and
from volunteers, she'd gradually gain confidence. "As
I've explained, a nurse will come by your apartment this
afternoon to get things organized. Some of our hospital
volunteers are going to be relieving you for a few hours

a day for the next few weeks. Do you have the schedule I gave you?"

The girl waved a sheaf of papers. "It's in here some-where with all the hospital forms… I think. Otherwise, I have no idea where I put it."

Irritation surged inside Sam. She'd put a lot of effort into helping Candy. The least the girl could do was hang on to her paperwork.

That wasn't fair. Candy's system must be flooded with hormones and she faced a tremendous amount of adjusting. Regretting her moment of impatience, Sam asked, "Do you want me to come by tonight?"

"No, thanks," Jon said. "A bunch of my friends will be coming over to play with them."

That didn't sound like a good idea. "If you'll check the discharge instructions, you'll see that newborns are very vulnerable to infection. Especially during flu season, we recommend that only family interact with them."

He drew himself up, offended. "My friends aren't in-fected with anything."

Sam reminded herself that these babies belonged to their parents now. She had to let them go. "Just be careful."

The young man appeared to teeter on the edge of argu-ing, but Candy's warning glance apparently dissuaded him. "Okay, maybe just a *few* friends. And they'll wash their hands and wear those paper masks the nurse gave us for visitors."

He was showing better judgment already, Samantha reflected. Lots of new parents were young and inexperi-enced. "You'll do fine. I'll see them for their checkup on Friday, okay?"

Candy nodded and, at her signal, a volunteer pushed the elevator call button. While they waited, Sam gazed down at the little ones. She sympathized with Connie as the underdog, but Courtney's intense expression gave the impression of a little mother hen in the making.

Of the trio, Colin had the strongest grip on Sam's finger and held her gaze for a fraction of a second longer. She'd have sworn he recognized her, but then, why shouldn't he? She'd spent a lot of time around the babies since their birth.

But they weren't hers anymore. Never had been, really.

Then, with the whisper of wheels and the brush of footsteps, they were gone, the double doors closing out her last glimpse of the group.

Samantha stood clenching and unclenching her fists, feeling ridiculously bereft.

MARK FOLDED AWAY HIS CELL phone. There went a perfectly good Saturday afternoon golf game. Tony, the hospital attorney had cancelled to spend the day with his fiancée, planning their wedding. Earlier, Jared Sellers had begged off in order to fill in for an ailing colleague who was signed up to perform newborn hearing and vision screenings at a health fair.

An afternoon on the links would have provided a welcome release after the week's pressures. Mark supposed he could show up at the course and join some random group, but once strangers found out he was a doctor, they tended to interrupt his concentration asking for medical advice.

Rounding a corner in the hospital hallway, he paused at the sight of Samantha, shoulders slumped and strands of hair escaping her ponytail. Although she stood in front of the elevator, neither button was lit.

The events of this week obviously weighed on her. He wished she didn't have to deal with that business about the counseling clinic on top of her medical issues.

When he started forward, his footsteps rang out. At the sound, Sam's spine straightened.

Mark drew alongside. "Up or down?"

Her puzzled glance resolved into a look of understanding as she eyed the buttons. "Down."

He pressed.

"Don't tell me you're done for the day," she said. "So early? Oh, wait! Golf with Tony, right?"

"He cancelled. Sellers, too."

"Poor Mark. Abandoned by your friends."

"You don't play, do you?" That would be almost too convenient. Mark suspected Sam would golf with the same fierce competitiveness she displayed in her work. Still, he'd be willing to give it a shot.

She shook her head. "Never learned."

"I could teach you."

The elevator opened. "Thanks, but I'll pass."

"Such gratitude," he kidded as they got in.

"I am grateful. To be alive and healthy." She didn't sound very happy, though.

He was well aware of Candy's release a few minutes earlier, since he'd signed off on her medical condition. The departure of those three precious little ones had clearly added to Sam's slump. "You think those kids will rise to the demands of parenting?"

"I have to hope so. Candy's a good person underneath, but she comes from a dysfunctional background. She tends to be impulsive and short-tempered, and so does Jon." Samantha blew out a long breath. "All the more reason to have people around them who will offer support rather than criticism."

Her comment reminded him of his sister. "I grew up with people who wreaked havoc and left it for others to clean up. Support is fine, but there have to be limits."

"I probably set those limits a bit further out than you do." They emerged on the first floor and headed toward the staff exit. "But I'm not an enabler, if that's what you think."

An enabler, in substance-abuse terms, was a person who helped a loved one continue self-destructive behavior by easing or removing the consequences. "There's a fine line between enabling and caring," he told her. "I ought to know. I've crossed it."

"You?" Her eyebrows rose. "You never seem to have trouble enforcing the rules."

Mark preferred to keep his family troubles private. Still, Samantha had wept in his arms and shared her grief. Plus, he could use some objective feedback about his sister. He'd spent a lot of time since yesterday thinking about her call.

"You walking home?" he asked. Although he didn't recall Sam's address, they occasionally arrived on foot at the same time, so her house must be close by.

She nodded.

"Mind some company?"

"Not at all. And I promise I won't harangue you about work unless you deserve it, which depends completely on you."

"I promise to be utterly blameless and saintly," Mark announced as they walked past the parking lot.

"Sounds boring." Her mouth curved in an impish grin.

There was nothing boring *or* saintly about his reaction to that teasing smile. For the sake of his own peace of mind, Mark seized on the first neutral topic that occurred to him. "How are plans coming for the Christmas party?"

"I have volunteers handling the decorations and the

music. The theme is 'A Hot and Happy Christmas'—carols set to a salsa beat, Santa draped in a red-and-white serape. You'll be there, right?"

He nodded. "I may bring a guest."

Sam missed a step. He caught her arm as she stumbled, holding her tightly until she regained her balance. The sudden motion sent a few more wisps of hair tickling around her forehead. Irritated, she yanked on the covered elastic as if to pull it off. Instead, it stuck fast.

"Ow!" She added a few pediatrician-appropriate swear words, "Doggone! Blast it," while pulling on the rubbery cord. All she achieved was to get the thing tangled even more tightly in her hair. "I should have just left it alone. Now it's stuck. Got a pair of scissors?"

"You aren't going to cut off your beautiful hair, are you?" he asked in dismay. There went one of his favorite fantasies, the two of them entwined in bed with Sam on top, blond waves curtaining him.

Just as well. He normally made a point of *not* fantasizing about anyone he worked with.

She winced. "No, I didn't mean for my hair. I need to cut off the elastic."

In his pocket, Mark's hand closed around his multi-function pocketknife. Not only could he snip the elastic, he could uncork a wine bottle, file his nails and probably shoe a horse if he really had to. But he'd much rather spend time talking to Sam than leafing through medical journals, so…

He slipped an empty hand out of his pocket. "I have several pairs of surgical scissors at my house. I suspect that's pretty much en route to yours. And I happen to stock excellent coffee."

Sam regarded him speculatively. "Any chocolates?

I passed up having a muffin with my friends. Now I'm feeling deprived."

"I have a box in the freezer. Several, in fact." Patients went overboard at holidays with gifts of candy, which he saved for special occasions. "I'd like to use them up before the next round of gift-giving."

"Dark chocolate with nuts?" she queried.

"Plenty. Just don't mess with my caramel centers."

"I wouldn't dream of messing with your caramel centers." She gave her hair one last tweak. "I can't fix this myself, so you're on, Doc."

Taking this desirable woman home with him might not be the wisest move he'd ever made, Mark reflected as they set out again. But for some reason, he felt reckless enough to find out what might happen when he did.

Chapter Five

Samantha had no idea where this other woman had come from. Not the one Mark might be bringing to the Christmas party—she refused to yield to the jealousy-tinged curiosity nipping at her about *that* individual—but the one she herself had become. She'd walked into Mark's large cul-de-sac home, surveyed the spare, clean lines of his living room and immediately pictured it stuffed with her flowery sofa and chairs, along with her collection of colored glassware.

"That's the real problem," she said aloud.

Beside her, Mark pulled off his tie and tossed it over the back of a modern chair so low it nearly didn't *have* a back. He ignored the way the tie slipped onto the seat. "What, exactly?"

"I'm not sure who I am anymore." There, she'd put into words the issue that had been driving her crazy.

"Well, that's a relief." He tossed his jacket after the tie.

As it slid down, too, a trace of his ubermasculine pheromones wafted toward her. Sam could have sworn her brain was floating a few inches above its usual position. "Why?" she managed to ask.

He sent her a lazy grin. "I thought you were about to comment that I decorate like a guy who ran through Ikea throwing items into a shopping cart. Which is basically what happened."

"It's nothing a froufrou addict like me couldn't fix," she said, distracted by the possibility that he might actually enjoy having some of her stuff…no, wait. Back to reality.

"So what's this about not being sure who you are?" He swung a leg over the arm of the couch and sat there, invitingly rumpled.

"I felt impatient with Candy, who's just a kid, after all. I keep thinking about the children I *should* have had, instead of about the counseling clinic. It's like I've turned into a…what are these for?" She stopped pacing to study the sleek, ash-colored cabinets built against one wall. Why had Mark outfitted his living room as if it were a storage facility?

Unable to resist, she opened one. Empty.

Sam couldn't imagine owning cabinets like these and not filling them up. The world was full of so many pretty things.

"They came with the house," he told her. "I only bought it a couple of years ago. Haven't had a chance to put my stamp on the place yet."

"It has your stamp on it," she shot back. "A stamp that reads, Nobody's Home."

His expression turned mischievous. "Is that any way to talk to the man who's going to be holding a pair of scissors close to your hair?"

"I should call Kate."

"Tony's fiancée?"

"She's also my hairdresser, or used to be."

"You don't need a hairdresser—you need a shrink," he observed with a twinkle in his eye.

"Because I'm having a crisis?" She hated feeling

disheveled and out of sorts while Mark remained maddeningly cool. "Which you helped cause."

He raised his hands in protest. "You're not the only person with goals and dreams around here, Sam. Besides, you've always known that the fertility center was the hospital's priority. Your project was a mere afterthought."

He had a point, one she didn't feel up to debating, not in her light-headed condition. "You promised to feed me."

"Are you certain you want to risk eating here? Remember Greek mythology. If you eat or drink anything in Hades, you may be stuck there forever."

"You're crazy."

"But fun to be around."

Someone had to wipe the amusement off his face, so Sam did the only thing she could think of. She walked over and kissed him.

He caught her arms and anchored her there. What started as a gentle exploration deepened, his tongue catching the edge of her teeth, her hands sliding across his shirt and feeling the rise and fall of his chest.

He did some exploring of his own, thumbs tracing the edge of her breasts and smoothing across the swell to reach the hard nubs. When she arched instinctively, he tasted the pulse of her throat, and her blood turned to steaming lava.

Speaking of a hot Christmas, this was quite a preview… or was she having a hot flash? That unpleasant prospect thumped Sam out of her trance. Come to think of it, all of her symptoms might be due to menopause. Wooziness, loss of concentration, cravings…

She retreated beyond the reach of his arms. "Well, that cleared my head."

He studied her questioningly. "My head doesn't feel clear at all."

Her breasts ached for more of his touch, and her lips tingled. "I think we went way off track there."

"Maybe we should try it again and see if it helps us find the right path."

She closed her eyes and registered the sensations rampaging through her nervous system. "I'm tempted, yes," she decided. "Insane, no."

"Samantha, did you have anything to drink this morning?" His joking manner shaded into wariness.

"Nothing stronger than coffee," she said.

"Are you taking medication?"

"I'm not high." She bristled. "Why would you even think that?"

Mark uncoiled from the sofa. "I apologize. The person I mentioned who might accompany me to the Christmas party is my sister, who's a recovering alcoholic. And frankly, I don't trust her claim about being sober. Guess I was projecting."

In fairness, he'd had good reason to ask. "I *have* been acting ditzy," Sam admitted. "And I'm sorry to hear about your sister. I had no idea."

"Lots of people have skeletons in the closet." He led the way to the kitchen. "My closet happens to be a veritable boneyard."

"Your closets were empty."

"My metaphorical closets are stuffed to the gills."

He'd always struck her as the soul of stability. "I thought your father was a doctor, like my folks. I pictured you growing up normal."

"And you consider physicians' children normal?" Although he'd turned away to measure coffee, the tilt of his head indicated he awaited her return volley.

"We may be a bit high-handed." She took a seat at the table. "Also impatient when a man *reputed* to be an excellent surgeon can't manage to extract a simple rubber band that's eating my head."

That remark brought a deep, rich laugh. "One band-ectomy coming up." After clicking the coffeemaker into action, Mark examined the contents of a drawer. He selected a small pair of sharp scissors and approached with caution. "I'm not used to doing this without a nurse. Perhaps a whole surgical team."

"I could give Lori a call."

"Too late." Setting the scissors on the table, he lifted the tangle of hair. With scarcely a tug on Sam's scalp, strong, deft fingers cleared away loose strands, freeing as much of the band as possible. The gentle strokes felt like caresses.

In the quiet room, she heard the rush of his breathing. Even facing away, she could detail the muscular length of Mark's body and picture the set of his jaw. She'd watched him perform surgery a few times on complicated cases, and she knew the intensity of his gaze and the way his lips pressed into a firm line.

Snip. One cut must not have been enough, because the scissors snicked again. Then, with the merest of pinches, he plucked out the remnants of the band, and thick waves brushed the nape of her neck.

"Good job," Samantha said.

"You haven't seen it yet."

"I can tell. You have talented hands."

"So I'm told." He came into view, discarding a pathetic clump of elastic and hair into a wastebasket. After washing up, he fetched a box of chocolates from the freezer. "These don't take long to defrost."

"Have you done this before?" she asked, bemused, as he took out mugs and plates. "Eaten junk for lunch?"

"I frequently eat junk for lunch."

"Just curious." Normally, she'd be on her feet, pouring coffee and helping set the table. But today, she felt an unusual lassitude, which translated into an inability to budge. "Just show me the contents, will you? Of your cabinets."

"My cabinets?"

"I'm curious. They aren't bare, are they?"

"Certainly not." Obligingly, he opened one. She cataloged a couple of china plates, neatly stacked, three cups bearing the logos of charitable organizations, four glasses and a lot of open shelving.

"That's disgusting," she said.

"What is?"

"Empty space. Don't you get a burning desire to swing by a yard sale and check out the goods?"

Coffee, chocolates and Mark joined her at the table. "I can safely say that urge hasn't seized me, not once."

"You're urge-free?"

"Of the desire to shop at yard sales? Yes." He studied her across the table. "Where do you find the time?"

"Mostly while I'm supposed to be exercising," she admitted. "Mark, do you want kids?"

His dark eyebrows met in the middle. "Are you offering to have my child?"

"As if I could." She shook her head ruefully. Why *had* she asked him that? Because, she supposed, she wanted to know more about him. Although they worked together and could probably finish many of each other's sentences, she hadn't been aware until today that he had a sister, let alone an alcoholic one.

"I'm doing the world a favor by not having kids."

What on earth motivated him to say such a thing? "You have to be joking."

He shook his head. "My genes are nothing to brag about. Neither is my schedule."

Sam thought this over. Not much to think about, really. "I vote for a world filled with miniature Mark Rayburns, as long as they don't kick poor patients out in the street."

"When have I ever done that?"

"Aside from the clinic?"

"Those aren't patients." He regarded her closely. "I know *you* wanted children, but have you truly considered what's involved? I'm not a hundred percent convinced you'd be willing to make the sacrifices."

She missed her mouth with the edge of her coffee cup, sending a shower of the brew onto her knit top. "Darn." She dabbed her chest with a paper napkin, keenly aware of Mark's interested expression.

"I'd be glad to help," he said with mock earnestness.

She wished her breasts didn't tighten beneath his gaze. "I'm sure you would."

"But that might be construed as harassment."

"I'm the one who kissed you," she reminded him. "Forget it. I'm working up some outrage and I'm not going to waste it by flirting." Deep breath. "How dare you imply I wouldn't be willing to sacrifice for motherhood?"

Whatever it took, she'd do it. When she was ready, Sam amended for the sake of honesty.

"I don't doubt that you'd sacrifice your comfort," Mark told her soberly. "And your finances, and possibly your health. What I meant was that I doubt you'd give up your volunteer work."

She'd never considered motherhood and volunteering incompatible. "Why should I?"

"Because children deserve more than spare minutes between working and saving the world, which is part of why I choose not to have any," he said. "And because *you* deserve the joy of being there for those unpredictable, precious moments when a child says or does or understands something in a unique way."

She didn't have to nurture her annoyance any longer; it sprang up forcefully. "There's no reason I can't manage all that."

"There are only twenty-four hours in a day," Mark cautioned. "And very few years before kids start sharing more with their friends and teachers than with their parents."

"A woman shouldn't have to choose between motherhood and other goals," Sam snapped.

"Everybody has to make choices. Men included."

This conversation wasn't going at all to her liking. Well, two could play at this game, especially since Mark seemed blissfully unaware of his own shortcomings.

"You make choices too easily," Sam countered. "You choose one course of action and push everything else aside without considering whether it's necessary or wise or *right* to compromise."

"That's rather a broad conclusion, don't you think?"

"But accurate." Sam believed in intuitive leaps. "You were quick to doubt your sister's sobriety."

If she'd expected an offended reaction, she'd have been disappointed. "I'd put the odds against her showing up for Christmas at eighty-twenty," Mark said levelly.

Samantha was rooting for his sister, and not only out of compassion. "I'll take those odds."

He tilted his head. "What's the bet?"

She hadn't considered this a real wager, but why not? As long as they kept things light. "A kiss under the mistletoe."

He gave her a heart-stopping smile. "Yes, but which of us gets the kiss?"

"You do, if you win." Sam would enjoy it, too, but she needn't mention that.

"What if *you* win?" he asked suspiciously.

She wanted to suggest he let the counseling clinic keep its quarters, but he'd never agree to that. "You buy me a piece of kitschy glassware at a yard sale." Not that she wanted any more clutter. Rather, Mark needed to loosen up. He might even decide to buy a few odds and ends for those nearly naked cupboards of his.

"It's a deal." He stood and reached across the table, and they shook. Big, warm hand with blunt fingertips, which struck Samantha as very masculine.

"Orange is a nice color, but I like blue, too," she advised him. "Multicolors have a kind of retro glamour."

"You're picky about your cheesy glassware?"

"Just the opposite," she said. "The bigger and more flamboyant, the better."

"You're pretty confident about winning."

"I have faith in your sister. I mean, she's related to you. Take it as a compliment."

"I'm trying," Mark said.

They sat contemplating their bet and stealing glances at each other. Sam couldn't recall the last time she'd relaxed like this with a guy. Male friends occasionally escorted her to charitable functions, and she'd had her share of lovers over the years, but they rarely seemed to find idle moments. Mark, she suspected, was not all that different. Yet here he was, and here she was.

"Why haven't you ever married?" she blurted. "Or did you, and I missed it?"

He pretended to wince. "Is this another of your stump-the-host questions, like whether I want children?"

"Is this another of your evasive answers?"

"I was engaged once," he said. "How's that for not being evasive?"

"You haven't filled in the details yet," Samantha pointed

out. While she'd assumed he'd had serious girlfriends, the news of a broken engagement surprised her. Mark seemed like the kind of guy who'd choose with care, and then follow through. "When?"

"A few years ago, in Florida." His shoulders hunched into what she interpreted as a defensive posture.

"Was it that bad?"

"What do you mean?"

"You're bracing as if…" She searched for a football analogy. "As if you're about to be tackled."

He lowered his shoulders, regaining control. "My fiancée was a nurse. Smart and fun to be around. And worth spending my life with, or so I believed."

"What went wrong?"

"She got caught stealing drugs from the hospital. Turned out she'd been addicted to painkillers since a car accident the year before."

His jaw tightened. What an ugly situation. While Sam sympathized with anyone struggling to work through pain and addiction, stealing drugs from the hospital where you worked was a serious breach of trust, as well as a crime.

"How awful. I presume she hadn't confided in you."

He shook his head. "If I'd known anything about it, I could have lost my medical license. I cared about her, but I felt betrayed, too."

"What happened?"

"I helped Chelsea get into a rehab program, but while I understand about addiction, I couldn't forgive the violation of trust. That was the end of our plans together."

"Being addicted and violating trust go hand in hand," Samantha observed sympathetically.

"As I learned growing up."

Her heart went out to him. "Which one of your parents? Not both, surely."

"Dad didn't abuse substances, but he had affairs. That can be an addiction in its own way. My mother drank herself into liver failure." He spoke tightly but without hesitation.

He'd come to terms with his loss, at least at some level, Sam gathered. That didn't mean he'd released all the anger or the pain.

"Do you blame your dad?"

He shrugged. "Did he cheat because she drank, or did she drink because he cheated? Maybe both, or maybe they were drawn to each other's dysfunctions."

That brought them to the subject at hand. "What about your sister? When did she develop problems?"

"She started binge drinking as a teenager. For years, I kept trying to save her, and kept failing." Sorrow shadowed his eyes. "Finally I had to admit defeat and let her go. Now I'm reluctant to buy into the same cycle of hope and regret all over again."

The rough note in his voice touched Sam. "She left scars."

"She did."

"Scars can be stronger than the tissue they replace," she noted.

"Other times, you have to cut out the scar tissue or it limits your ability to function."

"Is that why you're prepared to think the worst of her?" Sam probed.

"We'll see come Christmas, won't we?"

They'd finished their coffee. And, apparently, their conversation.

"We should do this more often," Mark said.

"With healthier food."

"Agreed."

Sam cleared away the chocolate wrappers and washed

her hands. It was hard to leave this place, warm despite its starkness, and this man who filled up a room with a subtle sense of power.

And yet, she reflected a few minutes later as she headed toward her house a block away, although Mark seemed contented, he didn't strike her as happy.

She had no idea what anyone could do about that. Oddly, though, she felt an urge to try.

Chapter Six

On Monday morning, between performing several C-sections Mark pondered Samantha's questions. *"Do you want children? Why haven't you ever married?"*

As a rule, he enjoyed his life. Got a jolt of adrenaline from planning the new fertility clinic. Relished bringing babies into the world and helping women lead healthier, fuller lives. And prized going home to a peaceful environment, without the drama, tears and temperaments he'd grown up with.

Today, though, he couldn't escape the image of all that empty space in his cupboards and cabinets. How did it feel to watch a woman arranging her colorful vases and bowls in there? To come home and cook dinner together, and talk over the events of the day? And, watching a new father's face light up as he held his son for the first time, Mark wondered what it was like not simply to appreciate the miracle of birth, but to know you were going to spend the rest of your life caring for that child.

Well, he planned to spend the rest of his life doing what he loved: using the talents and skills he'd been blessed with both as a doctor and as an administrator to make miracles happen.

When he reached his office, Mark listened to his voice

mail. One call had to be returned immediately. It was to Candy Alarcon.

"I'm sorry to hear you had a rough weekend," he told the young patient when he reached her. "If you felt it was an emergency, you should have called my service. They can reach me 24/7."

She heaved a long sigh. "Everything seems like an emergency these days, Dr. Rayburn. All these babies. Even with the volunteers, I feel overwhelmed, and now…" The sigh gave way to a sob.

Her message had mentioned postpartum depression, a matter that Mark took very seriously. While many young moms experienced brief episodes of sadness as they adjusted to their new role, serious cases of depression could interfere with the vital mother-child bond, or even stir suicidal thoughts.

If necessary, he'd prescribe medication, therapy or a combination of both. First, though, he needed to listen carefully to the patient.

"Can you come to my office in the medical building this afternoon?" Mark asked. "I'll clear time for you."

"How about right after lunch?"

He checked his schedule. "At one, Dr. Forrest and I are holding a press conference. Will four o'clock work?"

"I'm not sure. If my boyfriend…" In the background, a door slammed. "Jon just came home. I told him something I shouldn't have and now he's kind of upset. Can I call you back?"

"Sure. If you can't reach me, Lori will make an appointment. I'll let her know the situation."

"Thanks, Doc." The phone clicked off.

After a quick call to his nurse, Mark plunged into reading reports, advisories and updates about hospital affairs. He was immersed in the proposal for installing the basement lab when he got a call from Chandra in Louisville.

"What's this I hear about a press conference?" she demanded.

Mark gave a start. The vice president was nothing if not thorough. She must have scrutinized the hospital's schedule of events, posted on its website and updated daily.

"The counseling clinic is holding a Christmas fundraiser. That's all we're announcing," he assured her. "I have Dr. Forrest's word that she won't mention anything about the fertility center."

"Cancel it," she said.

"The press has already been notified."

"Then un-notify them. That woman can't be trusted not to shoot off her mouth."

Less than two hours remained until the event. While he understood Chandra's concern, Mark found it misplaced. "I doubt we'll be able to reach everyone in the media. In my opinion, it's better to go ahead rather than raise all sorts of questions about why we canceled. I promise I'll keep a lid on things."

"No offense, but you don't exactly have a shining track record for keeping a lid on Dr. Forrest," the veep replied. "I'm sorry I ever agreed to this counseling idea. I should have known it would be trouble."

"Trouble? I wouldn't say that."

Chandra cut him off. "I'm emailing you data about a major fertility conference scheduled for Los Angeles next fall. I want our new staff on board and presenting papers at that event. The prestige will be priceless."

"I agree. However, the organizers may already have scheduled the presenters," Mark warned.

"Then find out who they are and hire them," she snapped. "The fertility center is our number one priority."

"Of course."

"Don't waste your energy on distractions like Dr. Forrest's claptrap."

Samantha would hit the roof if she heard her pet project described as claptrap. But that wasn't the issue. "Even with a cancellation, we're going to have reporters show up. We'll have to tell them something."

"You should never have agreed to this," she said. "Make it go away."

No sense arguing further. "All right."

He put in a call to Jennifer in public relations. She told him what he already knew: it was too late.

"Do it anyway," he said resignedly.

"Okay. I hope you're wearing a hard hat and iron underwear, though. You know Samantha."

Oh, yes. Indeed he did.

It occurred to Mark that when he gave the go-ahead for the press conference, he and Sam had made a deal that effectively muzzled her. Now, thanks to Chandra, he was defaulting on his end of the bargain.

Maybe he'd better add a bulletproof vest to that list of protective gear.

WITH JENNIFER'S WORDS ECHOING in her ear, Samantha clicked off her cell phone. Her thoughts raced furiously. Apparently, she'd made a deal with the devil, and the devil had just reneged.

Sam refused to let her attraction to Mark interfere with her moral outrage. Nor would she yield to the fear of losing her job. Once she started censoring herself, she might as well give up.

This press conference was essential to notify the public about the fundraising event. Her center was losing its home, losing its cachet as part of the hospital and losing much of its momentum in the process. Without a boost at this critical point, it could easily crumble to nothing.

Dedicated as she was, Sam couldn't run a volunteer center on her own. She already counseled the group of teen mothers, and of course her medical practice took the bulk of her time and energy. She had to establish this center on firm financial footing. But how was she going to do that if she couldn't even reach out to the community?

Determination firing on all cylinders, she barreled into the nearest examining room, where two children stopped screaming at each other and stared at her wide-eyed. The little girl ducked behind her mother, who regarded Sam with relief.

"The sight of you puts the fear of divine retribution into them," the woman said admiringly.

"Now let's put the fear of divine retribution into that earache," Sam replied, and helped the boy onto the examining table.

By a little past noon, she'd prescribed antibiotics for earaches and ointments for rashes, completed well-baby exams, stitched a cut in a boy's forehead and persuaded a tearful mom to seek family counseling for her marital problems. Between patients, Samantha's outrage found its focus.

Despite Jennifer's attempts to call off the event, the press would be trickling in soon. The evil powers-that-be at Medical Center Management had seriously misjudged the situation, Sam mused with satisfaction as she took the stairs down. She'd corral the press in the parking lot and fire away.

The center had aroused widespread support in blogs and tweets and social media. While most of the donations that trickled in were modest, sometimes just a few dollars, they came from a significant number of individuals. The public appreciated this nonbureaucratic, caring attempt to reach out. Once reporters learned the whole story of the center's ousting, there'd be a firestorm.

Just what MCM deserved. As for Mark, he'd chosen his alliances. Despite a pang of concern, Sam refused to back down simply to spare him the embarrassment.

On the ground floor, she met up with Nora Kendall. The gynecologist pinned her with a glance. "How are you doing? I've been worried about you."

"The counseling center…"

"I'm talking about your health."

"Oh, that." Sam glanced around to make sure no patients were nearby. She preferred to keep her medical issues private. "Not sleeping terribly well," she admitted. "I've had a lot on my mind. I'm sure you've heard."

The other woman nodded sympathetically. "The hospital grapevine has been working overtime. I hope you locate new offices quickly."

"I suspect we're about to get a lot of support." Sam explained about the canceled press conference and the opportunity to make a public appeal, free of the restraint she'd promised Mark.

Alarm flashed in Nora's green eyes. "Hold on, Sam."

"Don't you start into me, too!"

"Just listen," the other woman said.

Sam planted hands on hips. "I'm listening. Talk fast."

"I realize that this feels like big business pushing around poor helpless women and kids," Nora began.

"That pretty much sums it up."

"You of all people should understand how it feels to have your chance at motherhood yanked away." She paused as a couple of pregnant women walked past, before continuing in a low voice, "The new fertility center will help people from all over the world."

Because many countries restricted treatments such as in vitro and banned others, including the use of surrogate mothers, couples flocked to California with its open policies. "I sympathize," Samantha said. "But when it comes to these high-tech procedures, we're talking about the wealthy."

Nora shook her head. "Not necessarily. I have patients of very modest means who're willing to spend every penny they can scrape together in order to have a family. And we'll be accepting a percentage of charity patients. Even the wealthy have hearts. Don't declare war on us."

Her use of the pronoun "us" brought Sam up short. She had been associating the fertility project so strongly with the corporate owner that she'd failed to consider the other stakeholders. Her fellow physicians. The patients. The babies that would come into the world loved and wanted.

"I can't just abandon…"

"No one expects you to," Nora said. "But don't take us down as collateral damage. You have a lot of power. The press loves you. You're famous."

"I am not!" Besides, what mattered was her cause, not her personality.

"The media makes instant celebrities, and you fit the bill," Nora countered. "Use your power wisely."

Things no longer seemed as blazingly clear as they had moments ago. While Sam hated shades of gray, the last thing she'd ever do was abuse power. "I'll try to temper my remarks."

"Try hard," Nora said.

A moment later, Sam emerged on the walkway. To her right, in front of the hospital, she spotted a TV van. She should be able to catch the camera crew before Jennifer sent them away. But what was she going to tell them?

THROUGH THE HOSPITAL'S front doors, Mark watched Samantha approaching. "Tell me this isn't going to be the shoot-out at the OK Corral," he muttered to Jennifer. Even though she'd done her best to call off the media, she hadn't—as predicted—been able to reach everyone.

The PR director's only response was an absent nod as she raced to wave down a camera crew. She also rounded up Tom LaGrange, a reporter for a local Orange County newspaper.

"I'm afraid we've had to call off the press conference," she was informing them as Mark came abreast. "The hospital *will* have a major announcement, hopefully in a few weeks, but there've been delays. I'm sorry I didn't get hold of you in time to save you a trip."

Hayden O'Donnell, an on-air television reporter, regarded her and Mark skeptically. "We understood the announcement involved Dr. Forrest."

"And here she is now," added LaGrange. He and the TV crew swung toward the pediatrician.

Mark had to concede that Sam cut a striking figure, her hair just wild enough to give her character, and her face alive with purpose. But apprehension took the edge off his instinctive pleasure at seeing her.

They were in for it now.

"Dr. Forrest." A microphone was thrust toward her. "What's going on? Is someone trying to muzzle you?"

Her gaze met Mark's. Despite everything that separated them, he felt a jolt of connection. And, amazingly, hope.

"I'm not sure what our PR director has told you so far," she began.

Jennifer seized her chance. "That the hospital isn't ready to make any announcement yet."

"That's right, although I would like to tell the public about our upcoming fundraiser." To Mark's amazement,

Sam spoke calmly, without a hint of defiance. "There'll be an open house from 2:00 to 4:00 p.m. on Christmas Day at the Edward Serra Memorial Clinic, on the fifth floor of the Safe Harbor Medical Center. Food, piñatas and entertainment. Our theme is 'A Hot and Happy Christmas.' Admission is free, but donations will be appreciated."

He began to relax. Was she really finished?

"And we'll be needing them now more than ever."

Oh, damn. To explain that ominous statement, Mark jumped in to run damage control. "People's generosity always gets stretched thin during the holidays, with so many appeals. Yet during the same period, stresses on families increase. The counseling clinic becomes more important than ever."

"Plus the fact that we have to move," Sam added.

Mark held his breath. If only they were in the auditorium, as planned, he could seize the podium and freeze her out, awkward as that might be. But here on the sidewalk, the reporters were free to ignore him.

Which they did.

"What do you mean?" O'Donnell demanded.

"Is the hospital kicking you out?" That was LaGrange.

"For the past few months, the medical center has generously allowed us to use an office suite free of charge," Sam continued into the microphone. "However, we've always known that was a temporary situation."

She hadn't grabbed the opportunity to bludgeon the hospital's reputation. Or was she building to an attack?

"After the first of the year, the Serra Clinic will need a new home. I appeal to corporations and other generous sponsors in the Safe Harbor area to contact me about any space you may have available free or at low cost."

Unbelievable. The outspoken Samantha Forrest had not only tempered her words, she'd cast the hospital in a somewhat favorable light. And refrained from putting the blame on the planned fertility center.

Jennifer blew out an audible breath of relief. Fortunately, the members of the press didn't appear to pick up on her reaction.

All the same, there was no mistaking the skepticism in the questions that flew at Sam. Both reporters demanded to know if she'd been pressured into downplaying the need to move.

She held fast. "We have the best interests of women and families in mind. No one's forcing us to do anything."

Crisis averted, for now. Mark could have hugged the woman. In fact, he hoped he'd get the chance. Soon.

"Looks like we're in the clear," he observed quietly.

"Uh." Jennifer's voice seemed to stick in her throat.

"Sorry?"

Wordlessly, she nodded toward the parking lot, where a van had pulled into the nearest handicapped space. A pudgy young woman with frizzy hair was unloading strollers with the help of a pregnant girl, probably a friend from the teen group.

Candy. He'd specifically requested that she come later, around four.

And, in the process, he'd told her about the press conference. Mark swallowed hard. How could he have forgotten that she was an even bigger drama queen than Sam?

Still, her motives might be innocent. "I'll handle this," he said, and set off to talk to his patient.

"Hey! Over here!" She waved at the press.

"Excuse me." Mark walked in front of her, trying to block their view. "I thought we were going to meet at my office," he said to Candy as quietly as he could.

"My boyfriend dumped me." Her lower lip trembling, the girl stepped around him. Raising her voice again, she declared, "This counseling stuff isn't all it's cracked up to be. Look at these triplets! I should have put them up for adoption, but Dr. Forrest talked me into keeping them. Now I'm stuck with three kids and no future."

"Of course you have a future," he told her, averting his face from the rapidly approaching reporters.

"Not since Jon left! You can't expect me to earn a living and raise three infants."

Sam had gone pale with shock. This had to hurt. Mark knew she'd been trying to meet Candy's needs, not browbeat the girl.

It was also ironic that just when Sam had moderated her pronouncements in the media, her old tactics were being used against her. Even worse, from the hospital's perspective, her attempt to paint Safe Harbor Medical Center as a sympathetic supporter of her project had just backfired.

Because if Candy succeeded in making the clinic look bad, so would everyone connected with it. Including the hospital.

And, Mark reflected ruefully, he'd be top of the list.

Chapter Seven

Had she really talked Candy into making a colossal mistake? Samantha wondered as the young woman and her friend lowered the triplets into strollers. She'd intended to help, not harm.

As she walked toward the new mom, she sorted rapidly through her concerns. For one thing, these newborns shouldn't be out in public, exposed to the gathering crowd of press and passersby. For another, what on earth did Candy hope to accomplish by attacking Sam and the counseling center?

Still, this was hardly the moment for reproaches. Clearly, Candy had suffered a blow.

Sam tried to ignore the riveted members of the press. "Why did Jon leave?" she asked. If this was simply a clash of temperaments, it might blow over.

Candy stuck her chin out. "What do you think? He's, like, twenty-one. You can't expect him to take on this much responsibility."

"Why don't we take this inside where we can talk privately?" Mark said. Sam could have hugged him.

"Why should I?" Candy replied. "I have nothing to hide." She turned one of the strollers to give a photographer a clearer shot of the baby. It was Courtney, her little face scrunched in the sunlight.

"That's too bright. It's hurting her eyes." Sam shifted the stroller. "Please, everyone, stand back. You don't want them to catch an infection, do you?"

The reporters shuffled slightly. Giving a few inches, at most.

"You said you'd told him something that upset him." Mark spoke in a level tone, his gaze fixed on Candy.

"I told him the truth."

"About what?" Sam hadn't suspected there was any hidden truth to reveal. The reporters leaned forward, trying to catch every word.

"That I got pregnant on purpose. I figured he'd marry me." The girl shrugged. "I wasn't counting on triplets."

O'Donnell broke in. "Did you have fertility treatments, Miss, uh—could you tell us your name, please?" He gestured for a crew member to hand the mic to Candy, which was, in Sam's opinion, akin to giving a hand grenade to a three-year-old.

Or to me. For the first time, she understood how Mark must have felt all those times when she had seized the floor.

"Candy Alarcon," the girl said. "No, I didn't need treatments. Twins run in my family. I just got one extra."

More people were gathering, attracted by the TV lights. "Everyone step back," Mark ordered. "As Dr. Forrest pointed out, these newborns are susceptible to airborne illnesses."

At his commanding tone, the onlookers scattered. Even O'Donnell retreated before Mark's stare.

"Let's go inside," Sam murmured.

Candy folded her arms. "No way. Look at that ugly Mark on Connie's face! It's still there."

The TV reporter perked up. "One of them has a birth defect?"

Sam was losing patience. "It's called a port-wine stain and we're planning to treat it. Connie is a wonderful child with a minor problem. Candy has no idea how lucky she is. Giving birth to three healthy triplets is a blessing."

"Lucky? I'm the victim here." Candy made sure the camera was trained on her before she added, "If people want to help, they can send donations to me. Candy Alarcon. I've set up an account at…"

"Shame on you!" To Sam's amazement, the words burst out of usually low-key Jennifer, who'd been doing her best to shoo away newcomers. "Exploiting these poor little babies when Dr. Forrest arranged for donations of supplies and services! What kind of mother are you?"

For a tense moment, Sam feared Candy would retaliate. The press would love an open battle. Judging by Mark's tense expression, she could tell he was thinking the same thing.

He'd been right, Sam realized. She should have stayed away once he called off the press conference. Matters always seemed to get too volatile around her.

"What are you going to do?" Tom LaGrange asked Candy.

"Are you filing a lawsuit?" added the TV reporter.

Did he have to bring that up?

While the young mother weighed her reply, Sam moved to check on the babies. Courtney was grumbling so low she could barely be heard above the ambient noise. Colin's mouth pursed, likely in search of a nipple. They needed to be fed. Connie waved an arm as if reaching for comfort. For her mom.

Never mind the hullabaloo. Sam yearned to gather them all close. They deserved responsible, caring parents. Why had she foolishly imagined that someone as immature as Candy would rise to the occasion?

Perhaps she'd projected her own feelings onto the young woman, imagining an inner strength that didn't exist. With the best motives in the world, Sam had done these infants a terrible disservice. How was she going to fix that?

The young woman's words broke into her reflections. "I'm going to give them up under the safe harbor law."

"Safe Haven," Jennifer corrected automatically.

"Are you sure?" Mark asked. "Candy, these aren't the best circumstances for making such a decision."

The girl stared at her infants. Courtney let out a cry, and Colin had started fussing. "I feel like I ought to love them, but I don't. Not like a real mom. I thought maybe if I had enough money or something... I was just mad at Jon. I'm sorry, Dr. Forrest. I know you were trying to help."

"But aren't you past the seventy-two-hour limit?" queried O'Donnell, his voice resonating as if he were revealing something of earthshaking importance.

"The what?"

"Under the Safe Haven law, babies can be surrendered with no questions asked if it's within seventy-two hours of birth," Jennifer explained.

Candy frowned. "How many days is that?"

"Three."

She stared at them in dismay. "You mean I'm stuck?"

Colin chose that moment to let out a piercing screech. His mother glared at him.

"Absolutely not." Sam didn't give a rat's tail about the camera swinging toward her or the fascinated observers still lingering around them. "You want to relinquish your babies for adoption? I'll be more than happy to take them. All of them."

"Even her?" Dubiously, Candy indicated Connie.

"Especially her."

"Can she just do that—give them to you?" LaGrange asked.

"It's called a private adoption," Sam told him. "It's more complicated than a Safe Haven relinquishment, but we can take care of all the legal requirements in due time. Right now, she's free to yield physical custody of the babies if she chooses to. What do you say, Candy?"

As she registered the girl's uncertainty and Mark's raised eyebrows, it occurred to Samantha that she might have spoken hastily. Three babies with her full schedule? Cribs and a changing table and all that other stuff wedged into her two-bedroom house with zero preparation?

None of it mattered. She loved these little ones. And she felt suddenly as if the events of the past week, from learning about her early menopause to her sadness at saying farewell to the triplets, had been preparing her for this moment.

If Candy agreed, Sam was about to become a mother. In triplicate.

CRAZY AS THIS WHOLE IDEA might be, Mark stood there silently rooting for Sam. If Candy had any sense, she'd accept the offer.

And if Sam had any sense? Well, that wasn't up to him.

"Okay," the girl said.

The press appeared at a loss for words. That didn't last long. "Tell me, Dr. Forrest," intoned O'Donnell, "exactly what are the differences between surrendering a baby under the Safe Haven law, and signing one over for adoption?"

She glanced past him. "I'll let our staff attorney handle that. Here he comes now."

Mark spotted Tony striding toward them. "That's good timing," he murmured.

Jennifer tapped her cell phone. "I called him."

"Thanks." He appreciated her efficiency.

As the press focused on Tony, Mark felt his concerns ease. He couldn't blame Sam for a colorful tendency to shoot from the hip. In fact, her knack for publicity would no doubt boost the fundraiser, and she'd handily deflected any negative impact on the hospital or the counseling center.

On the other hand, under the glare of the cameras, she'd just made a lifetime commitment with scarcely a moment's thought. Did she understand what she was getting into? While Mark had every respect for Samantha's pediatric knowledge, that didn't necessarily translate to a realistic understanding of parenthood. He might not be experienced in that regard, either, but he at least had the sense to recognize how much he *didn't* know.

Despite his impatience to talk to her, he paused to listen as Tony explained that before the Safe Haven law, a parent who dropped off a baby—even at a safe facility—and fled could have been charged with the crime of abandonment. The tragic result had been that women in desperate circumstances used to dump newborns in trash cans or other unsafe places. Now that they could leave them at a designated hospital or fire station without the risk of charges, far more babies were being saved.

Still, it was better if the mother stayed long enough to provide a medical history and sign legal papers, Tony told them. That way, the infant could be placed for adoption without an investigation to ensure the child hadn't been brought to the drop-off location by an unauthorized person such as a babysitter.

"What about the triplets?" the TV reporter asked. "They're over the time limit."

"Their mother isn't abandoning them, so she hasn't violated any laws," Tony continued. "She's free to relinquish them for adoption by signing the appropriate documents. The adoptive parent or parents must file a legal petition with the court and undergo a home study to make sure they can provide a suitable environment for the child or children. I'll assist Dr. Forrest in making those arrangements."

"Doesn't the father have any rights?" LaGrange queried.

"That depends on the circumstances. We'll try to get his signature, but if he refuses to take responsibility for the children, that may not be necessary."

Reassured that Tony could manage the press under Jennifer's watchful eye, Mark slipped away to join Sam, who was shepherding Candy and the babies into the hospital.

He took her aside. "Everything under control?"

She pushed back a flyaway twist of blond hair. "I checked, and the center's day care has space for them. They'll stay in the isolation room today while I'm at work." That was where employees' children were housed when ill. "In a few days, they should be fine in the regular infant section."

"What about after hours?" Mark asked. "They'll need attention at night, and you have to sleep."

Her gaze bored into his. "Are you lecturing me about my health, Doctor?"

"I'm lecturing you about your common sense, Doctor," he answered in the same half-joking tone.

Wrong tactic, he realized as she drew herself up. "My common sense is fine, Mark. It's my nerve you're doubting, isn't it?"

"Your nerve is the one thing I've never doubted."

She chuckled. "I'll choose a better word. My *resolve*."

"I've never doubted that, either."

"Good." She flashed him a grin that was too contagious for his own good. "Connie, Courtney and Colin were meant to be my children. Don't you see how everything's come together?"

Her early menopause, the delivery of the babies and Candy's very public decision to relinquish them… "What I see is a series of coincidences," he warned.

"One man's coincidence is another man's destiny," she returned. "Or woman's, in this case. By the way, you've heard of night nurses, right?"

"Yes, but I've also heard that they expect to be paid." While she earned a respectable salary, Mark knew she was far from wealthy.

"My grandparents left me an emergency fund. I've always felt it was there for a reason, and this is it."

That took care of one obstacle, but despite her take-no-prisoners attitude, Sam didn't possess superpowers. "You're well organized, I grant you. But raising three infants can be overwhelming. For anyone."

"Yeah." Without his noticing, Candy had joined them. "I think it's great that Dr. Forrest's going to find out exactly what she wished on me."

"Whoa." Sam regarded the young woman in mock dismay. Or perhaps it was real dismay. "Is this your notion of revenge?"

"You have no idea what my last two nights have been like." Candy held up one hand. "Okay, that's not fair. I *did* think it would be cool to keep the babies, back when they were inside me. My friends encouraged me, too. Plus I had this dumb idea Jon would act like a real father."

Sympathy softened Sam's features. "I'm sorry I didn't prepare you better for the reality. I got carried away with my own fantasies, I'm afraid. But what about your mom?"

"She was helping me last night and all of a sudden she burst into tears. She said she likes the idea of grandchildren, but she's only forty. She wants to have free time with Jerry, not spend every spare minute changing diapers." The girl swept a rueful gaze toward the strollers being piloted toward the day care center by hospital volunteers. "If you'd told me it was a bad idea, I wouldn't have believed you."

Sam gathered her into a hug. "You still have to get back on your feet. You'll come in for counseling, won't you?"

"Oh, yeah. And my friends in the teen group are sticking by me. I kind of wish I could keep one baby, but that wouldn't be fair. They belong together." Candy ducked her head. "Besides, those cribs and stuff are taking up all the room in our place."

"If it's okay, I'll borrow them temporarily," Sam said. "Then I'll pass them on to the other teen moms."

"Cool."

Tony came indoors, moving with an easy stride. Newly engaged to Kate and the happy father of a baby girl, he'd shed his former air of tight control. "Jennifer's finishing up with the reporters. Would you two ladies care to step into my office?"

"You and Candy get started with the paperwork," Sam said. "I'll be right up after I check on the babies." And off she went.

"She's a...what's the word?" Candy asked.

"Force of nature?" the attorney supplied.

Mark had nearly said "maniac." He was glad he'd thought better of it.

Sam had an iron will and an office lined with documents attesting to her pediatric expertise. But three babies at once? Whatever happened next was sure to be interesting, Mark mused.

He'd better go put in a call to let Chandra know that the press conference cancellation hadn't come off as planned.

By a rather wide margin.

Chapter Eight

"Forgive me for being an interfering mom, which I swore I'd never do, but are you certain this is a good idea?" The image of Dr. Lanie Forrest on the computer screen might lag a bit, and her voice sounded fuzzy over the internet connection, but her folded arms and creased forehead spoke volumes to her daughter.

"I never thought I'd hear negativity from you of all people!" Sam fought down the impulse to cross her own arms.

"Just because you agreed to take them, that doesn't make the decision irrevocable on your part," added her father, Dr. David Forrest. His thin face was filled out by a salt-and-pepper beard. "Not that I'm suggesting you renege on your decision, honey. But this is only the first step in a long journey."

"You mean life?"

"I mean the legal system."

That was true. According to Tony, Sam had to wait a month and undergo a home study, then appear in court for a judge's final approval. None of that mattered. From the moment she'd promised to care for the babies, they'd become hers.

Sam didn't kid herself that, even with her emergency fund and her determination, she'd have easy sailing.

Raising a baby, let alone three, would be a challenge for any single parent. Oh, heck, she had yet to come to terms with what was involved.

But she'd given her heart. That counted even more than giving a promise.

Determined to dispose of unnecessary tasks, she had thrown her stack of unread holiday cards into a box and instructed Devina to add any other personal notes to the heap. Usually she relished reading messages from former patients and coworkers, but they'd have to wait until she had spare time. Even if that took eighteen years.

She'd checked on the babies several times during the afternoon, and picked them up by 5:00 p.m. Lori had helped her install car seats in the van Sam had hurriedly leased with help from Jennifer, who'd also arranged to have Candy's cribs and other equipment delivered.

Where would a woman be without her friends? Nevertheless, Sam didn't like to depend on them any more than necessary.

Lori had stayed to help feed the infants, leaving a few minutes ago, shortly before 7:00 p.m. Regrettably, they had to rely on formula, but then, Candy had mentioned that she already used it as a supplement. While it was possible for a mother to nurse triplets, it took time and practice.

Breast milk offered many advantages, including the mother's immunities and nature's intended balance of nutrients. But adopted infants generally thrived on formula, and Sam planned to keep a close watch on the babies' development.

The night nurse she'd hired would arrive about ten. So here she sat in front of her computer, cradling a baby as she related the day's events to her parents several hundred miles south in Mexico.

"How are you feeling?" Lanie put in. Her graying hair, once blond like Sam's, had taken on a wiry quality.

"A little tired," Sam admitted. "That's to be expected until we settle into a routine. I'll try to have a nurse on hand until they can sleep through the night."

"That may take longer than with singletons," her mother warned. "They'll tend to wake each other up."

"If that becomes a problem, I'll keep a crib in my room." For now, Sam had turned her home office into the triplets' bedroom, and the furniture crowded around her with narrow passageways in between. Good thing she didn't mind clutter. "I could move another one into the living room at night."

"Great! Then you can run an obstacle course from room to room to room," Lanie grumbled.

"Mom!"

"You're such an overachiever. I hope you won't feel like you have to stick with this if it wears you out."

"Lanie," Sam's dad said in a warning tone.

Time to change the subject. "How're things at the clinic?" she asked.

"We finally got enough flu vaccine for everyone in the area." As hoped, the question distracted her mother, and the rest of the conversation centered on the couple's efforts to improve the health of local residents.

Their village sounded like a warm, caring place. If Sam ever did decide to join them, she'd bet her kids would love it there.

Her kids. What a beautiful term.

Afterward, Sam remained in her desk chair with Courtney dozing against her chest. The little girl smelled sweet and fresh, and from this angle it was amazing how long her lashes looked against her rounded cheeks.

She put Courtney to bed, then studied each of the infants

in turn. How precious they were in their footed sleepers, tiny fingers flexing, little bow mouths pursing as they dreamed their baby dreams. In the stillness, she listened to the murmur of their breathing.

For the first time since the press conference, Sam had a moment of actual peace and quiet. It felt like an unbelievable luxury.

The doorbell rang.

She jumped. The babies barely stirred, but she hurried to answer before it rang again.

Not the press, she hoped. O'Donnell had reported the story on the six o'clock news. With the TV playing in the background while she and Lori fed the triplets, Sam had caught glimpses of herself, Candy and the infants. The report had mentioned the fundraiser so briefly that most viewers probably missed it. Thank goodness the newspaper's website, which Jennifer had checked, cited the event prominently.

Reporters who'd missed the impromptu presentation would be trying to make up for lost time. Sam sure hoped some overeager newshound hadn't dredged up her home address.

She supposed she ought to drag a brush through her hair and put on lipstick. But if she stopped to do that, the fool might punch the bell again.

On the doorstep, she found a welcome surprise. Sam's frazzled nerves hummed harmoniously as she took in Mark Rayburn, tie askew and his jaw covered in five o'clock shadow, carrying a sack that smelled like heaven. Garlic, tomato sauce—Italian food. The scent reminded her that she'd missed dinner.

Sam didn't care what a mess she must look. "You were sent by the angels," she said as she ushered him inside.

"That's what I keep telling the corporate honchos. I don't know why they ever doubt it."

At the moment, Sam didn't know, either.

MARK FELT AS IF HE'D STEPPED inside a rainbow. Colored glass vases, candleholders and bowls filled china cabinets and spilled onto the coffee table and end tables. The shimmering effect reminded him of a cut-glass crystal vase his mother used to treasure—until she smashed it against the fireplace one night in an alcohol-fueled rage over one of his father's affairs.

"So this is what's meant by decorating," he said.

"You don't have to tell me it's overkill," Sam replied. "I'll pack the loose pieces away before the babies start crawling."

He hadn't meant to criticize. Best to let it pass. "I hope you're hungry. Papa Giovanni's makes the best ravioli this side of Italy."

"Starved. Right this way." Navigating between pieces of newly arrived baby equipment, she led him into the dining room, where she removed a stack of medical reports from the antique-style table. "I'll grab plates."

While she went into the kitchen, Mark lifted take-out containers from the sack. "I take it the babies are sleeping," he said when she returned.

"Dozing." She set out the plates and glasses of water she'd carried on a tray. "Don't try to be polite. Go ahead and tell me I'm a nutcase. I won't be offended. Much."

He helped place the silverware. "You aren't crazy. I love kids, too. In small doses."

She filled her plate from the containers. "Pardon me for being rude, but I'm starving. Aren't you?"

"The restaurant plied me with breadsticks while I was waiting for my order."

"Lucky you," she mumbled, and dived into her food.

During the meal, Mark took an appreciative look at the watercolor paintings splashed across the walls. A jacaranda tree abloom in lavender blossoms. A seascape carved by a bougainvillea-draped bluff. A waterfall creating its own rainbow. The profusion of colors soothed him.

"These are beautiful," he observed. "It's not what I expected to find in your house. Your offices are so Spartan." The one assigned to her in the hospital as head of pediatrics was practically bare. Her office in the medical building had a corkboard displaying photos sent in by happy patients, plus the expected medical certificates and professional awards. But nothing like this.

She gazed around. "This is my nest. When I was growing up, we lived like we were in the military. Nothing but essentials ready to pack at a moment's notice, although we stayed in the same house practically forever. My parents met in the Peace Corps in South America and they swore they'd be heading south of the border again soon. Twenty-odd years later, they went."

"You're making up for those bare surfaces," he concluded.

"It's more than that," Sam told him. "I guess I've been cramming as much as possible into every day and every inch of space. This past week, it hit me that I've been living as if the cancer might return any day."

"And you finally accept that it won't?" He hoped that was the case.

"I'm trying to accept that I have to live one day at a time like everybody else." She polished off a last bite of garlic bread.

"Let me know if you figure out how to do that," Mark said, "because I haven't a clue. I'm generally thinking at least half a step ahead."

"You never seem rushed."

"I put a lot of pressure on myself." As he spoke, he consciously relaxed his muscles. He'd been tense all day. First there'd been the press conference business, followed by his strained late-afternoon discussion with Chandra.

Her staccato voice still rang in his ears. She'd been upset that Samantha had spoken to reporters and displeased that the hospital was once again featured on the evening news for a reason other than its medical excellence. Mark had barely hung on to his patience with the woman.

She ought to trust his judgment. He'd made his share of mistakes, but so, he suspected, had Ms. Chandra Yashimoto. Besides, today's situation had turned out well, even if it hadn't been strictly on message.

"Rough day for you, too?" Sam asked.

Rather than dwell on his running skirmishes with the executive, Mark deflected the question. "Occasionally I fantasize about practicing medicine full-time. But then I'd have to work under some idiot administrator who forgets to put patient care first. Instead, I get to *be* the idiot administrator."

"You're not an idiot. Very often."

"Such high praise."

Sam gave him a wry smile through her water glass. "You were pretty darn cool out there in the parking lot."

"I admired the way you handled the press," he admitted. "You were doing great until Candy showed up. When you decided to take the babies, well, that was unexpected."

"To me, too." Her plate empty, she leaned back.

"Were you even considering adoption?"

"Yes, in the theoretical sense." Even after a full meal and a long day, her sharp features exuded restless intelligence. "I didn't imagine it could happen this quickly, with these children, but it seems almost destined."

"And now you're a mommy." Mark found the term endearing when applied to Sam.

Emotions flickered across her face. "Oh, wow, I *am*, aren't I?"

"This comes as a surprise?"

"I mean, of course I know I'm a mother. But I've been so busy putting out fires, I haven't had time to consider the big picture."

He'd suspected as much. "Which part hit you the hardest?"

"That the kids are going to be counting on me to be there for everything." She rested her chin on her palm. "For help with homework and heartaches, for Halloween costumes and Christmas dinners, for proms and college prep. What if I let them down?"

The responsibility *was* a lot to take in. "You don't think you're up to it?"

"I'm embarrassed that I encouraged Candy to take this on, for one thing," Sam answered thoughtfully. "Today it was all I could do to get them fed and diapered, and that was *with* Lori helping. On Saturday, you told me a child deserves attention for those special moments. What if they all fly by and I'm too busy dealing with daily battles to meet the kids' emotional needs?"

He'd harbored those same doubts when she took the triplets. Yet Sam wasn't giving herself enough credit. "There's a bond between you and them. I saw it at the hospital."

Tears glimmered in her eyes. "I love them. When they cry, I feel how much they hurt. When I was working today, there was always a tug, always an awareness, like wishing I could be two places at once."

"I see my patients juggling and balancing the same way," he told her. "It's stressful, but they pull it off."

"But they have husbands. Sometimes grandparents living close by. A support system." Weariness frayed her voice. "I'm out here on the high wire alone."

Her unexpected vulnerability aroused Mark's protective instincts. "I can help. I'll be your backup."

She regarded him skeptically. "What do you mean by that?"

What *did* he mean, anyway? At a whimper from the bedroom, Mark paused, bracing for a cry while he collected his thoughts. The cry never came—the baby must have been fussing in its sleep—but a disturbing thought did.

He felt a powerful urge to cuddle and watch over those little guys. He'd followed their growth from early pregnancy until he'd lifted them from their mother's womb. They almost felt as if they belonged to him, too. But they didn't.

Raising these children was Sam's commitment, not his. He'd come dangerously close to promising more than he should.

Chapter Nine

"You're going to be my backup?" Sam prompted, the corner of her mouth twitching. "This I'd like to see."

Mark chose his words carefully. "I'll pitch in during this neonatal period, until they get stronger. You could obviously use the help." That seemed a reasonable way to see her through this crunch without glossing over the serious issues involved in raising triplets. Sooner or later, she was going to have to make hard choices about her priorities.

"Pitch in how?" Sam pressed. "Details, details."

"Since I live so close, why don't I stop by before work to help in the mornings?" *And play with the babies.* Impulsively, he added, "We could walk them to the hospital together when the weather's nice."

"That would be wonderful. You're great with kids, even if you have sworn off fatherhood." Her brilliant smile made him glad he'd volunteered.

"Before I forget, there's one more important matter to deal with."

Her smile frayed around the edges. "You're not kicking the clinic out before Christmas, are you?"

"Nope." From the Papa Giovanni's sack, Mark retrieved another white container. He flipped the lid to reveal two slices of Italian cake dipped in espresso, layered with a sweet creamy mixture and topped with cocoa. "I was referring to dessert."

"Tiramisu!"

"My way of leaving a sweet taste in your mouth." His gaze flew to her lips. Mmm. He'd definitely like to leave a different kind of sweet taste in her mouth.

"That's fantastic. Thank you."

Better to make an escape while he still had his wits about him. Mark pushed back his chair. "The cake's for you, so enjoy it whenever you like. It's been a long day, and all good things must come to an end."

"Must they?" she broke in teasingly. "You could rub my shoulders. You did offer to be supportive, right?"

He ought to beg off. Common sense, good judgment... oh, the hell with them.

"So I did." Without giving himself any more time to reflect, Mark moved to stand behind her and ran his thumbs across the ridge of her shoulders. "You're knotted up." Sam was as tense as if she'd been carrying the weight of the world.

Her hair drifted across his hands. "Hauling babies and gear does that to you."

He kneaded the lines of tension, probing between her shoulder blades, exploring her spine. A sigh fluttered from Sam. Her scent drifted upward, the sharp tang of antiseptic softened by baby powder and herbal shampoo and a whisper of femininity. She held so much in check, but now, in this moment, Mark felt her relax against his hands, against him. Satisfaction pulsed through him that he could ease her tension and cares. A healing power flowed from him into her.

Glancing down, he saw her eyes drift shut. "You going to sleep?" he teased huskily.

"Dreaming. Fantasizing. Don't stop."

His mind kept veering toward some fantasizing of its own. Firmly, Mark focused on working out the nubs and knots in Sam's shoulders. The two of them shared a great deal, but he didn't kid himself about their fundamental differences. There was a line he refused to cross, no matter how much he might be tempted.

Yet when she tilted her head back, lifting up her sleepy face, he bent and traced a kiss across her temple. "You *are* going to sleep."

"Think how much easier it would be to help in the morning if you stayed here all night," she murmured.

Mark's body hardened at the suggestion. *And I wouldn't sleep on the couch, either.* With an effort, he dragged himself back to reality. Or, at least, to pragmatism. "Me and that army of nurses you hired?"

"Only one. Did you have to remind me?"

He chuckled and couldn't resist adding, "Besides, you'd regret that offer."

"What offer?"

"The one you just made."

She twisted to look up at him. "What did I say? I was half-asleep."

"You propositioned me."

Her mouth dropped open, but she rallied. "Well, good for me."

"Because sex would relax you?" He quirked an eyebrow.

She brushed her palm across his scratchy cheek. "I give you more credit than that, Doc."

At the inviting touch, he instinctively pressed a kiss into her hand. As if he didn't know better. As if the two of them weren't like gasoline and a lighted match.

With a wrench, Mark pulled away. "Give me credit

for leaving while I'm ahead. I'll drop by in the morning around, say, six?"

"Perfect." Sam shifted as if to rise but couldn't seem to muster the energy. "Did you say *all* this tiramisu is for me?"

"Every last bite."

"You're a generous man."

"I'll remind you of that next time we cross swords," he said.

"I'll pretend I don't hear you."

She remained at the table while he wended his bemused way through a living room still reflecting prismatic rainbows from the glassware. He was closing the door behind him when he heard a wail from deep within the house and the instant response as Sam leaped from her chair.

A mother's instincts trumped exhaustion. Whatever he might think of her impulsive decision to adopt, Sam had obviously given her heart to those babies.

ON TUESDAY MORNING, MARK arose half an hour earlier than usual. After a shower and breakfast, he scanned his personal email, as was his custom. A sale at the golf pro shop…updates from former coworkers at his Florida office…and a funny photo from Bryn of a startled-looking puppy and kitten, curled in each other's paws and staring at the camera as if they'd been caught in an indiscretion.

Hope your day is full of unexpected moments read her message.

Failing to think of a clever response, he typed, "Can't wait to see you. I miss your sense of humor. Love, your bro."

Maybe Sam was right and he should have more faith in his sister. People did overcome substance abuse. Due to the drug thefts, his former fiancée had been unable to find another job as a nurse, so she now worked as a reception-ist and volunteered at a homeless shelter. Recently, she'd messaged that she and her new husband were planning to start a family.

If Chelsea had shaken off the demon of addiction, Bryn could, too.

Showered, shaved and ready for the day, Mark tossed an old work shirt over his clothes as protection and headed toward Sam's house. He arrived at the bungalow to see the night nurse, a middle-aged woman in a pink uniform, heading for her car. "How'd it go?" Mark asked.

She peered at him dubiously. "Excuse me?"

He hadn't considered the disreputable effect of the torn shirt lumpily covering his suit. "Dr. Mark Rayburn. I promised Sam I'd stop by. How's everyone doing?"

"The triplets are fine, and Dr. Forrest got a few hours' sleep," the nurse summarized. "I tried to let her rest, but someone forgot to tell the babies to take turns getting hungry."

"Thanks for the report." He categorized Sam's first night with the babies as provisionally positive, since no one had fallen ill, but the situation sounded far from ideal. Concerned about the effect of inadequate sleep on Sam's volatile temper, he tapped cautiously at the door.

To a greeting of, "It's open!" he turned the knob.

From a blanket spread on the floor, the baby girl with the port-wine stain—Connie—blinked up at him. Beside her, a red-faced little boy was grunting mightily. The smell confirmed Mark's suspicions.

"Hi." Sam appeared from the hallway with a welcoming grin, Courtney at her shoulder. "I'm nearly done feeding her and then I have to dress." A shower-damp spiral of hair hung over one ear, and without makeup her eyebrows disappeared at the edges. Yet, to Mark, she seemed radiant.

And, amazingly, not at all crabby. The woman seemed to thrive on motherhood.

"Where's the diaper changing station?" He indicated Colin on the floor.

"No room for a changing table," she responded. "I use the dryer."

"Seriously?"

"It's in a nook off the kitchen. There's a pad on top and diaper supplies above on the shelf. Hey, that's one of the practical tips I give the teen moms. It really works."

Mark collected the little boy and carried him to the dryer. As he bent to his task, the little one's alert gaze followed him. "Remember me?" he asked Colin. "I'm Dr. Rayburn, but you can call me Mark."

A burbling noise might have been an attempt at communication, although it was too early for the kid to start babbling. The tiny mouth formed an *O*. Or, perhaps, a *D*.

"Daddy? Sorry, no." He felt as if he was letting the baby down. "I'm sort of a father substitute."

Blink. Stare. Yawn.

"Am I boring you?"

Colin studied him as if trying to puzzle out his meaning. Or perhaps marveling at how swiftly and efficiently the doctor changed his diaper, Mark mused.

The job finished, he lifted the clean baby. One wriggle, and the diaper slid down to half-mast.

So much for efficiency.

No wonder Lori always tightened the tabs after he examined a baby, Mark thought with a touch of embarrassment as he pulled the diaper more firmly into place. Thank goodness no one had observed his mishap.

Good thing babies didn't swap stories about their caretakers' dumb mistakes.

After returning the little boy to the living room, he washed his hands. He hadn't paid much attention to the strollers the other day, but a quick glance revealed a double and a single. Mark opened them and was positioning the second baby into place when Sam breezed out, smartly clad in a pantsuit with a receiving blanket safety-pinned to one shoulder.

"Thanks for helping with the strollers," she told Mark, and laid Courtney in the single pram. "Ready?"

"You don't waste time." He'd expected her to take another ten minutes at least.

"The only way I'm going to survive is to put myself on a supertight schedule," she informed him as they maneuvered the strollers outside, with Mark handling the double.

"I thought you were already on one."

"I play hooky once in a while, but I won't be able to do that anymore," she told him. "You were right—I'll have to give up a few things. Hanging with my friends, unless I can bring the kids. Browsing yard sales. Unnecessary stuff like that."

"That's how you recharge. You need to do those things." He paused to tuck in Connie's quilt. The temperature was in the fifties, crisp but not uncomfortably cold.

"I'll recharge by enjoying special moments with my children," she replied.

"Are those on your schedule, too?" He let her move ahead, since the sidewalk wasn't wide enough for both strollers side by side.

"Sure. I'll see them before work, pop in during lunch, and of course there'll be evenings and weekends." Her voice drifted back. "Except when I'm tied up with the counseling clinic."

"You can't do everything."

"Why not? I considered giving up advising the girls at the teen center, but they'll love the triplets. Besides, that's how I met Candy in the first place."

"Sam," he began through gritted teeth.

"You think I'm overcommitted, don't you?"

Since she'd brought it up, he saw no reason to soft-pedal. "You're going to crash and burn. Dial it back for a while."

"Like you?" she challenged. "Dr. Workaholic? You even delivered Tony and Kate's baby on Thanksgiving."

"That's different."

"How?"

"My family doesn't need me, because I don't have a family." The statement gave him an uncomfortable twinge. The words seemed to echo down a long corridor into the future. "Besides, I do relax. I play golf."

"You call that relaxing?" Sam asked as a woman jogger veered around them and continued on her way. "That's exercise, not fun."

"I get fresh air and stay healthy," Mark argued. "Whereas you're sacrificing your sleep and your leisure. You should identify other activities to drop."

Sam swung around so fast he nearly ran the double stroller onto her heels. "Quit harping on how overworked I am."

He *had* sunk to nagging. "Not another word," Mark promised.

She resumed course. Two minutes later, she halted to confront him again. "Quit thinking about my schedule."

"Excuse me?"

"I can feel your criticisms smacking me in the back like BB pellets."

"I was thinking about *my* schedule," he countered.

"No, you weren't," she blazed.

"You can't read my thoughts."

"They're written all over your face."

"You can't see my face—I'm behind you," he pointed out, and then wondered how he'd become entangled in such an absurd argument.

Sunshine highlighted the freckles sprinkled across Sam's nose. "I can read your thoughts from two floors away. Or even in another time zone, and you can do the same with me. You knew precisely how I'd react when you canceled the press conference, didn't you?"

If they kept arguing, they'd never get to work. "Maybe, but I gave you the benefit of the doubt."

"You did?"

"I might have upped my life insurance, but I trusted you to handle the press wisely. And did my best to stay out of it, honestly."

The crease eased from her forehead. "Thanks. Sorry for being so pugnacious."

"No problem." If he mentioned her lack of sleep, it would only make her temper flare again, so he kept silent.

Courtney let out a high, thin cry. Sam hurried to adjust her blanket, and then set out at a faster clip.

When they reached the medical complex, Mark realized how much he'd enjoyed the walk. He'd never known that a squabble could clear the air and bring people closer, yet in a funny way, that's what had happened. In fact, the experience had put him in an upbeat mood for whatever the day might bring.

Then he spotted two news vans parked in front of the hospital and a knot of reporters gathered on the walkway. What on earth was this about? "Any idea why they're here?"

"I guess I should have returned my phone messages

last night," Sam said wryly. "Apparently the triplets and I make a great human interest story."

Annoying as he found the press's intrusion, Mark didn't blame her. "I doubt a few phone interviews would have stopped them from showing up."

She adjusted her suit jacket. "Well, brace yourself."

He did his best.

Chapter Ten

As she endured a photo op on the hospital's front steps and answered questions about how the triplets had spent the night, Sam reminded herself that the news coverage was sure to boost support for the Christmas fundraiser. Honestly, though, did the woman from an L.A. paper have to keep asking her to turn Connie to make the birthmark more prominent? And if that radio reporter kept implying that Sam was only taking the triplets as a publicity stunt, she might deck him.

"That's enough," she was relieved to hear Jennifer announce. "Dr. Forrest needs to get the babies settled and she has patients to see."

"They aren't going to keep showing up, are they?" Sam grumbled as Jennifer and Mark provided a protective escort into the lobby.

"Depends on whether it's a slow news day. Pray for a Hollywood scandal." Her friend took over the double stroller from Mark, who departed with a wave.

Watching his jaunty stride as he crossed the lobby, Sam wished she could time travel back to last night's dinner. Having Mark in her house had made everything feel more grounded, more secure. Then this morning a zip of appreciation had run through her when she saw him with Colin. He handled the baby differently than she did, yet with great tenderness. Was it possible babies craved that fatherly touch?

Or that *she* did? When she awoke this morning, her bed had felt wide and lonely. Crazy. She liked having all that room to herself.

Busy wheeling a carriage down the corridor, Jennifer didn't appear to notice Sam was lost in thought. Thank goodness.

At the day care center, Jen planted a kiss on the baby girl she'd recently adopted. Rosalie's birth mother, anguished because she couldn't keep her baby, had seen the public relations director interviewed on the internet and chosen her to be the new mom. Then Jennifer had fallen in love with Ian Martin, the pain-in-the-neck reporter who kept splashing her and Rosalie all over the web, and—not being entirely an idiot—he'd fallen in love with Jennifer, too. Married a little over a month, she and Ian doted on each other and on their new daughter.

A day care worker hurried over to take charge of the triplets. Sam surveyed her to rule out any sign of illness, then yielded the little ones with a tug of mixed emotions.

Colin had already gained two ounces, she'd noticed, when she weighed him this morning. What if being left with a stranger put him off his bottle? As for Courtney, she was peering about with the usual worried furrow between her tiny eyebrows. And Connie seemed so vulnerable.

"Call me if they feel hot," she warned.

The worker fixed her with a knowing smile. "Thank you, Mom. Now it's time to leave."

"That's Dr. Mom. And I'll go in a minute. I'm not sure they're ready."

The woman planted her hands on her hips. "Don't you mean when you're ready? Dr. Forrest, I've been doing this type of work a long time. I know separation anxiety when I see it."

"Me?" Sam asked in astonishment.

The woman gave a knowing nod.

"Right," Samantha said, and tore herself away.

Was that a heartbroken cry from Colin? she wondered as she marched away. No, that screech came from a toddler whose toy had just been snatched by a preschooler.

And I thought my pediatric training gave me an edge on this mom business.

Sam found Jennifer waiting by the door. "Listen, I have an idea about the press," her friend said as they exited.

"Good. I've got more than enough to handle without them." How ironic that in the past, Sam had rather enjoyed talking to the media. Now she disliked having them dog her footsteps, or stroller tracks.

"Once the public's curiosity is satisfied, they'll turn to other things." Jennifer kept pace along the corridor. "Ian still does the occasional interview for Flash News/ Global."

He'd covered an international beat for the syndicate until signing a book contract to write about medical advances affecting women. "So?"

"Ian mentioned he'd like to discuss the counseling clinic with you, so why not let him write about the babies, as well? Video, still photos, the whole shebang. His stories go all over the world. That ought to slake people's thirst for triplet news."

Sam paused in a corner to let an employee in a wheelchair scoot past. "What did you inhale for breakfast?"

"Excuse me?" Her friend regarded her in surprise.

"You're usually such an expert, Jen, but *more* publicity? Next you'll be proposing I star in a reality show."

Jennifer tapped her foot angrily. "That's insulting, Sam."

Perhaps she *had* gone too far. "I'm sorry. But I'm also right. Think about it."

"It was a spur-of-the-moment idea. Forget I mentioned it." Her friend took a deep breath. "Changing subjects here, I have some good news about the clinic. Ian may have found a sponsor. She's dynamic and well connected, and she's looking for a project to pour her energies into."

"To raise funds for—that kind of thing, right?" Not a do-gooder socialite who wanted to play at actually running the place, Sam hoped.

"I'm sure she'd be more involved than that." Jennifer didn't seem to pick up the warning note.

"An amateur who jumps on every health care trend that comes along? Or a control freak who never met a piece of paperwork she didn't love? Email me with the details and I'll check her out."

Jennifer bristled. "Sam, the clinic doesn't belong to you. It's named after *my* son. You decided to take on three babies, which I applaud you for, but you can't keep the clinic under your thumb forever."

"I don't plan to. Once we've found new quarters and a professional director, I'll be happy to let go." Overjoyed, in fact.

"Without help, you may never be able to afford a director," Jennifer answered tightly. "This clinic means as much to me as it does to you. I was thrilled when Ian said he had a patron in mind."

Sam had already done more than enough arguing for

one morning. Besides, she valued Jen's friendship. "Let's table this discussion, all right?"

"Fine. But not for too long."

"I'll get back to you. I promise. And I do appreciate how much you and Ian care about the clinic."

All the same, uneasiness dogged Sam as she made her way to the medical building next door. She wasn't trying to hang on to the clinic. She simply refused to see it follow the same misguided path as the medical center itself.

Once a full-service community hospital, Safe Harbor had been converted into a facility primarily serving women and their babies. While that wasn't necessarily a bad thing, it meant taking in fewer charity cases and reaping larger profits. She understood the financial realities involved. For heaven's sake, she'd remained here in part because of her own financial realities—paying off medical school debts.

As for the counseling clinic, she'd established it as a place where women and families could drop in without worrying about who qualified for what or whether they played nice with an intake counselor. What about the cranky, the messy, the offbeat clients who didn't "show" well in front of bureaucrats?

Sam had worked too hard to get this place off the ground. She wasn't about to let it become a plaything for rich dilettantes who acted noble while serving only the right kind of clients, the ones who looked good on posters and appeared suitably grateful.

True, she couldn't hold on to the reins forever. But she didn't intend to let her new status as a mother stampede her into abandoning her vision.

OVER THE COURSE OF THE WEEK, to Mark's relief, press interest was deflected by the birth of twins in Los Angeles to a 60-year-old mother who'd been an Olympic gold med-alist. Controversy swirled over the mom's age, but her unusually strong physical condition and determination to have children qualified her for special consideration, according to the world-renowned fertility expert who'd helped her conceive.

The expert, Dr. Owen Tartikoff, flew from his home base in Boston to congratulate his patient and appear on several newscasts. A man of strong opinions—some called him abrasive—he was scheduled as the keynote speaker next fall at the fertility conference that had drawn Chandra's interest.

To his gratification, Mark managed to arrange a private meeting, at which he described the plans for the new fertility center and attempted to recruit Dr. Tartikoff as its director. Intrigued by the idea of building his own program from scratch, the man agreed to further discussions.

That would be an incredible coup. Yet, for now, Mark had to sit on the possibility. Aside from informing Chandra and Tony, he couldn't mention the matter to anyone. If word leaked out prematurely, it would be awkward for Dr. Tartikoff's current employers and might even kill the deal.

As for Sam, she continued her jam-packed schedule, putting in extra hours the following weekend to make sure she had the fundraiser well in hand. In the mornings, when Mark walked to work with her and the babies, she seemed as alert as ever, and insisted she'd slept plenty even though the night nurse advised him privately that Sam caught at most five hours.

He could see for himself that she was pushing too hard. The next time he brought food, Sam thanked him and spent the rest of dinner poring over reports on her laptop, keeping up with her position as head of pediatrics. When he asked why she was so determined not to let up in any area, she brushed aside his concerns.

"That's just who I am," she insisted. "If I'd wanted an easy life, I wouldn't have gone into medicine."

That attitude wasn't unusual among doctors, Mark had to admit. He'd observed surgeons ignoring their bodies' demands while performing complicated operations that lasted more than a dozen hours.

We expect too much of ourselves. Wasn't he almost as bad, seeing patients, performing surgery, running a hospital and getting up early to help Sam bring the babies to work? The busy schedule energized rather than drained him, but then, he was getting sufficient rest.

The next Friday morning, eight days before Christmas, Sam snapped at him for bumping the stroller too hard on their walk. "I hope you're planning to take it easy this weekend," Mark responded. "You're worn out."

From the fiery look she shot him, he expected an argument, but she apparently reconsidered. "I *am* kind of tired. I've arranged for a sitter to come in tomorrow afternoon so I can sleep and catch up on my bills."

"Put the emphasis on the sleep," Mark warned. "I don't want to pull rank, but if you're worn to a frazzle, I'll have to insist you take leave from your hospital duties." Her work with private patients lay beyond his control, however.

"You wouldn't!" She swung around on the sidewalk.

"Your behavior is becoming obsessive." Until he spoke the words, he hadn't fully realized that was the case. "It's almost as if you're addicted to adrenaline."

"I've always been addicted to adrenaline." Her voice had a ragged edge. "So are you."

"You rest tomorrow and Sunday, too. If the sitter lets you down, call me."

"What? No golf?" It was the closest she'd come to teasing him in days.

"Tony, Ian and I are playing tomorrow," Mark conceded as they resumed their pace, Sam leading the way. "But I'll have my cell with me."

She shook back her hair. "Lori's swinging by in the morning. We'll be taking the kids on a stroll and to our coffee klatch. But after the sitter arrives, I promise to hit the hay."

"Glad to hear it."

He didn't remind her that the clinic was running out of time to find new quarters, because the last thing Sam needed was more pressure. Jennifer had mentioned a potential sponsor, which sounded terrific, except that so far Sam hadn't pursued the matter. Mark supposed he could stall the corporation until the end of January. But no longer.

He'd really like to offer more help. When it came to obsessive behavior, though, hadn't his experiences with his sister taught him that more was never enough?

Sooner or later, Sam had to face reality. *That* would be the time to step in and help sort things out.

PLAYING GOLF SLUICED AWAY the pressures and concerns of the week. Although Mark wished Samantha had agreed to let him teach her how to play, he enjoyed being out here with his friends, too.

He loved the pine-scented air of the golf course, the steady, unhurried pace, and the excitement of each hole when the possibility of a perfect shot—a rare hole in one—loomed as a distant but achievable moment of glory. He'd scored a couple of them over the years, mostly through luck, but the joy remained brighter than any trophy.

As Tony collected his ball at the last hole, Mark didn't

mind that his score, while respectable, left him behind
his two companions. He'd fallen in love with the sport as
a teenager, when it was the only thing he and his father
shared. If not for golf, he'd have grown up scarcely knowing Dr. Robert Rayburn. And although Mark always played
with a competitive spirit, he'd been glad that he occasionally lost to his dad, because the man seemed mellower
when he won.

After moving to southern California, Mark had tried
skiing. For a while, he'd driven to the nearby mountains
at least once a month during the winter and occasionally
in summer for a change of pace. He'd even bought a cabin
there as an investment. Now he mostly kept it rented out by
the week, because after the initial challenge, he'd returned
to his first love.

Golf.

At the nineteenth hole, as the on-site restaurant was
termed, the men discussed the latest football results over
buffalo wings and beer. "I'm hoping to score some press
tickets to the Rose Bowl," Ian said. "As a special treat for
Jennifer." The game was played on New Year's Day in
Pasadena, about an hour's drive from Safe Harbor.

"You're sure you won't be wasting them?" Tony asked.
"Most women aren't that crazy about football."

"My sister's a big soccer fan." Ian's twin sister lived
in Belgium with her husband and kids. His family had
moved all over the world as they were growing up, Mark
recalled.

"Well, Jennifer isn't your sister," Tony pointed out. "Did
you ask her?"

"If she turns you down, I'll go," Mark volunteered.

"Lucky man. You don't have to check with anyone,"
Ian said. "Not that I envy you being single."

"Wouldn't have it any other way." And yet, oddly, Mark

felt a hollow twinge as he said that. New Year's Day...he *had* no plans. What would Sam and the kids be doing?

Sleeping, he hoped.

"Take Jennifer to the Tournament of Roses Parade instead," advised Tony, the only one of the men who'd grown up in southern California. "You have to practically spend New Year's Eve waiting on the sidewalk to land a good position, but those floats are fantastic up close. And you can attend the game later, if you do manage to get tickets."

"I'll look into it," Ian promised.

"Oh, wait," Tony said. "Forget the sidewalk. There's VIP seating. If you have enough pull to get tickets to the game, I'll bet you could get some to the parade, as well."

"I'll *definitely* look into it." Ian turned to Mark. "By the way, did Jennifer talk to you about Eleanor Wycliff?"

The name rang a bell. "Isn't she the widow of that federal judge who died while under indictment for bribery?"

"Technically, she isn't his widow—they were divorced," Ian said. "But that's right. I interviewed her about the case a few months ago, just before he died."

The man had succumbed to a heart attack, Mark recalled. "What about her?"

"Their seventeen-year-old daughter, Libby, took her father's death hard, as you can imagine," Ian explained. "Eleanor's wealthy, and she's been looking for a project that she and Libby could work on together, not just a charity to throw money at, or a place to serve hot soup on holidays."

"How'd she get interested in the clinic?"

"She heard on the news about it having to move and remembered that it was named after my wife's son," Ian replied. "She's eager to serve on the board, except that we don't have a board yet."

"Sounds promising."

"It would be, except that Sam practically bit Jen's head off when she mentioned I was talking to a sponsor." Ian shrugged. "Jennifer thinks she can't bear to lose control."

"Especially not to some amateur. Isn't that how she put it?" Tony must have discussed this with Jennifer, too.

"How did I miss all this?" Mark wished he'd paid more attention to the PR director's comments.

"You've been busy," said his sympathetic staff attorney.

Mark shook his head. "Not that busy." How frustrating for Ian to find a backer, only to run into Fortress Samantha. In her physical and emotional state, she might be turning down the clinic's salvation. Did she have the right to do that? "I'm not even sure who the clinic belongs to."

"It's not incorporated," Tony said. "It belongs to whoever funds and operates it."

"Up to this point, that's been the hospital," Ian put in.

"Sam would disagree," Mark said. "She believes it's hers. Besides, the hospital has no interest in holding on to the clinic."

"Well, my wife has strong feelings on the subject," Ian returned tightly.

Squabbling between Jennifer and Sam could only hurt both women as well as the clinic. Besides, once Sam caught up with her sleep, put Christmas behind her and had to stare eviction in the face, surely she'd be more amenable to the offer. Especially if they paved the way diplomatically.

"Here's an idea," Mark told the other men. "Ian, why don't you invite Mrs. Wycliff and her daughter to the fundraiser? Perhaps they could take an hour or so out of their Christmas plans to stop by and meet Sam."

"To discuss the clinic?" the writer asked.

"She might mention her interest, but ask her not to make any specific proposals yet. This is just to break the ice. I have a feeling that seventeen-year-old girl will melt Sam's heart." Mark hoped so. "I'd like this to feel like a partnership rather than a coup."

"Sensible," Tony agreed.

"Mrs. Wycliff is a bit of a powerhouse," Ian warned. "She's used to having her own way. But she's done a lot of organizational work with charities before. I'm sure she knows how to smooth things over."

"Excellent." Mark's cell rang. Not surprising, given the unpredictable nature of childbirth. In fact, he'd enjoyed more uninterrupted time this afternoon than usual. He answered, "Dr. Rayburn," and hoped this wouldn't be an emergency.

Turned out that it was. But not the medical kind.

Chapter Eleven

"She's having a meltdown," Lori gasped into Mark's ear. "I've never seen Sam carry on like this."

"She's supposed to be resting." Surely the sitter should have arrived by now.

"Resting?" his nurse went on. "She didn't even get to finish her coffee this morning. There was supposed to be a Christmas party for those teen girls she counsels, and it got screwed up, so somebody begged her to rescue them."

"She isn't a party planner," he growled. Sam should have better judgment than to take on such an unnecessary task.

"I think it was Candy who called," Lori admitted.

Sam obviously felt an obligation to the triplets' mother. "What happened?"

"Sam insisted on picking up party platters and decorations. She had the triplets with her, so of course I helped."

"Thank you." He hoped Sam appreciated her friend's dedication.

"During the party, Candy started acting possessive about the babies, and she and Sam had some kind of blowup. Candy stomped out, complaining that they were her kids—it was scary. Then we got home late and the sitter had given up waiting and left. Sam's in a foul temper, the babies are crying, and frankly, I'm fed up." Lori's voice broke. "She accused me of being bossy and interfering. *Me!* I'd walk out, but I hate to leave the kids. I'm not sure Sam's up to coping with them right now."

Nearly two weeks of sleeplessness and too much work had finally pushed her over the edge. Somebody had to call a halt to this downward spiral, and like it or not, Mark was elected, both as hospital administrator and as Sam's friend.

Suddenly, he got an idea. Not merely an idea—a potentially dangerous but irresistible plan.

He was going to stage an intervention.

SAM COULDN'T STOP PICTURING the horrible moment at the party when she'd realized Colin was missing. Earlier, she'd seen Candy playing with him, so, trying not to panic, she'd gone in search of the young mother.

After another girl reported seeing Candy take the baby out of the community center, Sam had hurried to the parking lot. There, she'd spotted Candy preening in front of a tattooed, long-haired man astride a motorcycle. Cradling Colin in the crook of his arm, the man stood there revving his bike as if about to shoot into gear.

Sam didn't remember exactly what she'd said, but she'd grabbed the baby away and given both the man and Candy a piece of her mind. Unbelievable, to expose a fragile infant to exhaust fumes, germs and the possibility of being driven unsecured on a Harley.

Candy had pouted and declared that the babies belonged to her. As if they were possessions. As if she hadn't signed them over to Sam.

But she could still take them back. And now, she might, although for today she'd backed off.

Since their argument, Sam's emotions had been roaring

around like a lion in search of prey, ready to pounce on anything that moved. She regretted venting at Lori. Her friend hadn't spoken to her in more than half an hour since then, and who could blame her?

If only Sam didn't feel strung as tight as a wire, she might be able to focus her thoughts.

Pacing through her house, holding Courtney and a bottle that the agitated baby refused to suck, Sam seemed unable to calm down. From a bassinet, Colin's hungry cries scraped on her nerves. At least Connie, settled on Lori's lap, appeared to be taking her formula.

Lori. Today, her friend had done far more than Sam had a right to expect. "I'm sorry I overreacted."

"You freaked out." Lori's hazel eyes regarded her accusingly.

"I apologize. For everything. My rotten mood. My ingratitude." She hoped that wasn't too little, too late. "By the way, who did you call earlier?" She'd heard Lori talking on the phone, but hadn't caught the gist of the conversation.

"Jared. And…" The nurse bit back whatever she'd started to reveal.

"And who?"

"I called my ex-fiancé to come over and help with the babies. Isn't that enough?"

"And who else?" Suspicion threatened to overbalance Sam's delicate restraint. "Lori, you have no business going behind my back."

"You aren't rational today."

"I'm rational at an elevated hormonal level, that's all. Early menopause combined with unplanned motherhood."

"Is this a new medical condition?" her friend grumbled. "It sounds more like an excuse."

"And a pretty poor one, at that." Although Samantha

intended the remark to be humorous, it failed to draw a smile. Mercifully, though, Courtney began sucking at the bottle, and Colin's cries had subsided. Perhaps he'd fallen asleep.

At a knock on the door, Lori half jumped from her seat. "I'll get it." She took Connie with her.

Sam drew in a deep breath. If her friends could watch the babies for a while, she might be able to sleep. Or, more important, call Tony for advice about heading off any attempt by Candy to assert her rights. The worst part was the acknowledgment that girl was so irresponsible, she shouldn't be allowed *near* the triplets, let alone have a chance at reclaiming them. If Sam hadn't been so blindly optimistic, she'd have faced that fact months ago and helped Candy arrange...

What? A home for the triplets with a two-parent family? But then Sam would have lost her chance to love and cherish them.

For once in her life, she wasn't sure what the right course would or should have been.

From the front doorway, she detected two male voices: Jared's light tenor, and a deeper tone that had an amazingly soothing effect on her. Rounding a corner, she got a clear view of the entryway. There stood Mark in slacks and a knit golf pullover, his powerful frame overshadowing Jared's slender build.

She could have sworn Jared and Lori wore guilty expressions. Mark looked determined.

She must be a mess, Sam reflected. But she was too tired to care. And glad as she felt to see him...everyone...she couldn't muster the energy to conduct a polite conversation.

"I already hosted one party today, so forgive me if I'm

not in the mood to entertain," she said wearily. "Thanks for dropping by, guys. Are you here to babysit?"

"Not exactly." Mark studied her with resolve. Why did she get the sense that he'd come here for a purpose? "Please hand Courtney to Jared."

His tone struck Sam as odd. Instinctively, she resisted. "She's doing fine. Colin's the one who needs to be fed."

"Let me see her, okay?" With a shy smile that made his mustache twitch, the neonatologist held out his arms. Puzzled, Sam yielded her little charge.

Mark kept his gaze fixed on Sam. "You know how much we care about you, right?"

"What?" Dazedly, she wondered if everyone was behaving strangely or if she was simply imagining it.

"You're one of the toughest, most accomplished people I know," Mark went on. "We're lucky to have you in our lives."

"Wait a minute." His words rang a bell. "This almost sounds like an—"

"But lately, you've driven yourself to exhaustion," he continued.

If she agreed with him, maybe he'd stop talking like a shrink. "I admit, I could use a few hours of sleep. Things went haywire today."

"*You* went haywire today," Lori put in.

"I need a nap," Sam conceded, again.

"You need a break," Mark said levelly. "A nice long one."

"In an institution with padded walls and locks on the doors?" she returned irritably.

"Do you honestly believe you're in any shape right now to be responsible for three infants?" Mark persisted.

"The night nurse will be here in…." How many hours? Seven? Eight? "Well, whenever."

"I'll arrange for her to come to my house," said Jared, who had tipped Courtney's bottle at a jaunty angle that the baby seemed to like.

"Your house?" Sam repeated dully.

"We'll set up a temporary nursery," Lori told her. "That way, you can get some uninterrupted rest."

And Candy wouldn't be able to find them, so there'd be no immediate confrontation. "Not a bad idea," Sam agreed. "I'll bring my sleeping bag."

Mark took her arm and steered her toward the bedroom. What was he doing? she wondered, feeling that she ought to shake him off but too grateful for his strength to react. "You're going to pack an overnight case. You won't need a sleeping bag but be sure to bring warm clothing."

"What's wrong with this?" Sam indicated the clothes she had on. "Okay, I may have spilled some formula on the sweater, but…"

"You aren't going to Jared's house," Mark told her as Lori retrieved Sam's keys from a hook. "They'll transfer the car seats, pack up the babies and drive them to Jared's. You're coming with me."

She blinked. "Mark, there's no reason for me to sleep at your house."

"We aren't going to my house." Holding her elbow, he spoke so close that his voice vibrated through her. "Sam, I don't want you driving and I don't want you staying alone. Accept my help, for once."

"But where—?"

"You'll find out when we get there."

They were running an intervention. Saving Samantha from herself. Any idiot—well, any idiot in the medical profession—could see that.

She didn't need saving. For crying out loud, *she* was the person who saved others. Like Candy, except that today

Candy had accused her of being selfish and manipulative. Like the counseling clinic, except that Sam still had no idea how to assure its future. Like the teen moms, except that all they'd done at the party was whine because she hadn't provided a live band.

How had things become so messed up?

Somehow, while these thoughts were rattling around her brain, Sam managed to stagger into the bedroom and stuff fresh clothing into a small suitcase, along with a few reports she'd been meaning to read. Ducking into the bathroom to grab her toiletries, she got a shock when a witch loomed in the mirror. Could this Medusa-like creature really be her?

She burst into tears.

The worst of it was that she had to sob without making any noise. Because if Mark heard her, he might storm in here, grab her pathetically wrecked self and haul her off to…where?

She couldn't bear it if he turned her over to a crew of rehab specialists who talked in the first person plural, as in, "Now, Samantha, *we* shouldn't take responsibility for the entire world on our shoulders, should we?"

Sam felt certain she would commit vicious and unlawful acts if anyone spoke to her like that.

Taking a deep breath, she recalled her mother's advice that when chaos threatened, she should start with the things she *could* control. So she returned to the bedroom, grabbed clean jeans and a clingy pink sweater, and went to take a shower.

While blow-drying her hair, she noted with approval that the sweater did wonders to emphasize her breasts. If she had to spend the weekend feeling like a failure, at least she could make Mark uncomfortable in the process.

In the living room, she found him sitting on the sofa,

feeding Colin. Significant amounts of baby gear had vanished, presumably into Lori's and Jared's cars. Outside, she heard them discussing the correct method of installing an infant seat in Lori's subcompact.

Startling, the things a neonatologist and a nurse didn't know, when they'd never actually had children.

"This is an intervention for *them*, right?" Sam joked. "To get them together?"

Mark didn't miss a beat. "You bet. It's like a soap opera in the delivery room these days, with his longing gazes and her red-rimmed eyes. This has to stop."

She set her suitcase on the floor and tossed a windbreaker over it. "Are we going somewhere on a boat? I should warn you, I get seasick."

"No clues." At a coo from Colin, Mark bathed the infant in a warm smile. "Are we done, little man? Ready for Doc Rayburn to burp us?"

Sam grimaced. "Do me a favor. No 'we' and 'us,' okay?"

"Why not?"

"Reminds me of the wrong kind of men in white coats."

Lori banged in through the door. "Jared's heading off with the girls. Is Colin ready for his close-up?"

"You really think this will work?" Sam asked.

Her friend regarded her with uncertainty.

"Exposing Jared to all these babies to turn him off having children," Sam clarified. "You should cancel the special nurse so he has to get up and down with them."

"I already did that while you were in the shower. Although not for nefarious reasons. I just didn't think we needed her." Cautiously, Lori asked, "You're not mad at me for calling in reinforcements?"

"I plan to make Mark suffer appropriately," Sam assured

her. "And I forgive you if you'll forgive me for calling you bossy. You never did accept my apology."

"I forgive you—even if you are overbearing and irrational," Lori said cheerfully, and scooped up Colin.

Mark collected Sam's luggage. She locked the house, Mark tucked her into his passenger seat, and off they went into the unknown.

The only explanation for her meekness, Sam decided, was that she truly had reached the end of her resources. Either that, or someone had drugged her.

On the plus side, she caught Mark stealing a peek at her sweater. She'd have teased him about that, but she couldn't keep her eyelids from drifting shut.

SAM FELL INTO A DEEP SLEEP that lasted the entire two-hour drive to the mountain community of Big Bear. Although Mark was relieved, he wished she didn't have to miss the gorgeous scenery. Late-autumn rains had transformed California's brown summer landscape into an explosion of wildflowers and greenery. As they approached the 7,000-foot level, pine trees scented the chilly air, and he turned on the car heater for the first time that year.

He could swear Sam's condition was improving already. The farther they got from Orange County, the healthier the color of her pale skin. As for the form-fitting pink top with its V-neck, did she have any idea how that affected a man?

He didn't intend to do a damn thing about it. This weekend was an intervention, not a seduction.

Luckily, the cabin hadn't been rented this week. Tourism was slow due to a lack of snowfall, even though many resorts offered artificial snow on their slopes.

Mark had a spare key, and he kept clothing and toiletries

in a locked closet at the cabin. He'd even arranged for a cleaning crew to tidy up after they left. The only catch had been the possibility that Sam might go ballistic.

Instead, she'd crashed. Still, he didn't kid himself. Once she awakened, he might face a battle royal, but surely she wouldn't insist on interrupting Lori and Jared's chance at reconciliation. Her comment might have been intended as a joke, but he wished he'd thought of that angle himself when he planned this intervention for Sam.

Mark turned off the highway and followed a route through narrow streets lined with tall pines. Every now and then, he glimpsed a flash of blue from Big Bear Lake below them, before turning onto a bumpy street where cabins lay at odd angles to accommodate the terrain. Unlit strings of Christmas bulbs swathed several of the houses, and on one lawn, a cartoon reindeer and a Santa stood poised for their turn to shine after dark.

While the sky was overcast, no wind disturbed the overhead branches, Mark noticed. Accustomed to southern California's mild climate, he hadn't thought to check a weather forecast, but he doubted they were in for anything severe.

Still, you never could tell.

He swung onto a gravel turnaround and braked to a halt in front of his A-frame. Rough logs gave the exterior a rustic feel, and pine needles crunched beneath his shoes as he stepped out.

Leaving Sam to sleep, he toted her suitcase inside and checked the place. As he'd hoped, the rental agency kept the kitchen stocked and the bathroom and bedroom prepared with towels and sheets.

Outside again, he paused to study Sam through the passenger window. Guiltily, he noticed that she'd huddled in the seat, hugging herself against the cold despite the jacket he'd laid over her.

He tapped the glass, then opened the door. Still sleeping.

"Sam?" Mark crouched beside her.

"Grrr." Was she snarling or shivering?

"Wake up. We're here."

"Beat it." Matted blond hair hid her expression.

"Are you talking in your sleep or giving me a hard time?" he asked.

"Both." She stirred and peered at him. "Where are we?"

"Mountains."

She inhaled. "Mmm. Chilly weather makes me think of hot cocoa."

"If you're willing to lurch a few yards, I promise you all the cocoa you can drink." The rental agency always laid in a supply of that after-ski essential.

Sam stretched and covered a yawn. Her movements dislodged the jacket and provided another tantalizing glimpse of lovely curves revealed by a top so tight-fitting it ought to be outlawed.

"Getting. Up. Now." She swung her long legs out of the car and fixed Mark with a steely blue assessment. "Tell me this isn't an institution for the criminally bewildered."

"It's my vacation cabin," he told her.

She tilted her face toward the sky. A white flake landed on her nose. "Is that snow?"

"Just a flurry." When Mark glanced up, a couple more flakes dampened his cheeks. "At least, I hope it's nothing more."

"We might be stuck here for a long time." Sam sounded merry. "I've never been snowbound."

Before Mark could protest that his schedule simply

wouldn't permit him to get stuck in the mountains, she trotted ahead of him into the cabin. For better or worse, he'd whisked her away.

And now he had to make the best of it.

Chapter Twelve

At this elevation, they were literally in the clouds, Sam saw as she turned in the living room and gazed through the A-frame wall of windows. Trees, lake, snatches of fog, drifting bursts of whiteness. This entire cabin might simply float away as in—what was that children's book she'd loved?—ah, yes, *Howl's Moving Castle*.

Impulsively, she headed up the narrow staircase to the loft, where a wide sofa bed faced straight out into the heavens. "I'm sleeping up here!" she called over the railing to Mark, who was prowling through the kitchen cabinets.

"There's no privacy," he said, straightening. "I put your suitcase in the back bedroom."

"You just want the loft for yourself."

"That, too." He considered her assessingly. "Let's play for it."

"Play what?" Sam's competitive instincts surged even before she heard the details.

"Scrabble?"

"I'm not a word person."

"Dominoes?"

"Sissy stuff! Got a couple of swords?" She'd excelled in fencing as an undergrad at UC Berkeley.

"How about wrestling?" he called back.

"Why, Mark, I didn't know you cared."

He had the grace to blush. "You're out of my weight class, anyway."

The altitude was beginning to offset the bracing effect of the cool air. Feeling slightly woozy, Sam descended. "We'll figure out the sleeping arrangements later. Where's my cocoa?"

"Gee, you're pushy." Mark grinned.

"You're the one who brought me here," Sam reminded him. "What exactly happens at this intervention, Doctor?"

"You leave all your cares behind," he said.

"Done."

"That easily?" Standing behind the counter that divided the kitchen from the living room, he produced a couple of mugs and a tin of hot chocolate mix. As he filled the cups, the casual slacks and pullover emphasized a ruggedly masculine build that Sam would definitely enjoy wrestling.

Tearing her thoughts away, she responded to his question. "Sometimes I feel like I absolutely have to fix things, get them right, save the world. To the point of collapse, as you've seen. But up here, I can't do a thing about any of it, so why worry?"

His forehead furrowed as he clinked around fixing their beverages. "You said you're an adrenaline junkie."

"Sometimes I need help breaking loose," she admitted. "Now that it's done, what's next on the agenda?"

"Whatever you want."

"Anything?" she murmured.

He paused with a spoon in his hand. "What would you like?"

A simple response sprang to mind. *You.* "There's one method scientifically proven to relax people faster than anything else."

She could see awareness dawn in the way his pupils dilated and his lips parted. "I don't think that's a good idea."

"You seemed interested enough the last time we were alone without the triplets," she pointed out. "When you saved me from being strangled by my ponytail elastic."

The microwave timer buzzed. "I seem to be rescuing you a lot these days."

"The way you rescued your sister and your fiancée from *their* addictions?" she prodded.

"I suppose there is some similarity." He set a steaming mug on the counter and located a tin of biscotti in a cabinet. "Except I didn't actually rescue my sister. She rescued herself."

"Yes, but you tried your best." Sam blew on the piping hot cocoa. "Your pattern is to get involved with troubled women, steer them in the right direction and then move on."

He didn't look pleased. "You think that's the way I treat people?"

She nodded, more to provoke him than because she really believed it. "Well, if you plan to dump me as soon as we get home, I hope you'll at least wait until we've had sex."

Mark gave a start. It was a good thing he'd only opened the microwave door and hadn't removed his cup, or she might have had to treat a burn.

Sam wasn't sure why she enjoyed teasing him. Partly, she refused to let Mark stick her in the category of damsels in distress. Also, her body tingled every time he came close, and she was tired of being celibate.

The silence didn't last long. "I may be attracted to women with addiction problems," he conceded, "but I refuse to get caught up in a destructive pattern of enabling them."

"You aren't enabling me," she challenged. "So you have nothing to fear."

"Oh? Who's been saving your bacon every morning, helping you get the triplets off to day care?" He stood across the counter, balancing on both feet as if ready to swat back whatever conversational ball she lobbed in his direction.

They'd bypassed fencing and wrestling in favor of verbal tennis. Perfect—Sam had finally found a sport she could play while snacking.

"That isn't enabling, it's helping," she said. "Being a mother is natural and healthy and wonderful. Besides, you're in love with those babies. Don't bother to deny it."

Crinkles formed beside his eyes. "They're adorable." His expression turned serious. "They're going to need a father. Have you thought about that?"

She'd like to steer this conversation back into more playful areas. "Are you volunteering?"

Alarm flashed across his face. Oops.

Sam reached out and cupped his wrist. "That was a joke, Mark."

"I know." He took a sip of his hot chocolate.

"Twice I've knocked you for a loop," she said. "Does that mean I win the rights to the loft?"

"We'll see."

Or they could share it. In her present mood, Samantha didn't mind the idea at all. Best to get started right now, because given her state of weariness, she was likely to fall asleep early tonight.

Too bad for this inconvenient counter between them. "About that wrestling match," she began.

He pinned her, not with his arms but with a glance. "Behave yourself, Doctor."

"Oh, all right." She stretched her legs along the adjacent stool and turned away to enjoy the sight of snow whirling outside. A naughty impulse prompted her to stretch languidly, giving him an excellent view of her breasts.

"Sam." The low note in his voice sent chills through her.

"Mmm?" She peered at Mark from beneath lowered lashes.

"I'm only human."

"That's what I'm counting on."

He gripped the edge of the counter. "I'm trying to listen to my better judgment."

"What happens in Big Bear stays in Big Bear," she said.

"Is that a promise?" He eased around the counter. Losing the battle? She hoped so.

His hand smoothed along her leg toward her thigh. Instantly, heat sparked through her body, firming the tips of her breasts and warming her right to the core.

"There's not much privacy in this room," Mark observed softly.

"From all those hordes of snow bunnies outside?"

"Why don't we…"

Her phone rang. They both froze.

"Couldn't you have brought me to a cabin without cell reception?" Sam grumbled.

"Don't answer."

"What if it's about the triplets?"

The tone sounded again. Sam wished she'd taken the time to program different ring tones for different people, so she'd know if it was Lori or the answering service or….

The display read: *Candy.* She showed it to Mark.

He nodded resignedly. With a jolt of fear at what the young mother might be about to say, Sam answered.

MARK WASHED OUT THEIR MUGS while Sam listened to her caller. He was grateful in a way for the interruption, because he'd been on the verge of yielding to his impulses. But would that have been so terrible?

It had struck him during their conversation that he'd been in an awful hurry to view Sam's behavior as addictive, to put her in the same box as his sister and his former fiancée. While her behavior could go over the top sometimes, did one weakness really erase all the strengths?

She needed a counterbalance, someone to rein her in when she went too far. Wasn't that what couples did for each other? Maybe he ought to take a risk, for once. And today, Sam seemed more than willing to meet him halfway.

This weekend had given them a rare chance to get to know each other...*if* Candy didn't drive Sam right back into a frenzy. And her reaction wasn't the only thing bothering Mark about this call.

Earlier, he'd been too focused on Sam's meltdown to reflect on Candy's possessive behavior toward the triplets, but if the teenager insisted, she still had the legal right to reclaim them. He'd always doubted the young woman's readiness to parent, and after what he'd heard about her behavior at the party, he felt even more certain it was a bad idea. Eventually, a social worker might determine negligence and take them away, but in the interim, there was no telling how much harm she could inflict.

He had a vivid image of Colin this morning, peering trustingly up while taking the bottle. The bond between child and parent had always struck Mark as an instinctive thing, predisposed by hormones and nature. But that didn't account for the tightening in his chest whenever he pictured that little boy and his sisters being hauled off by an immature, unstable mother.

Sam was pacing through the cabin, phone pressed to her ear. Mark tuned in to her remarks. "Are you sure you're all right?… Well, I *was* angry… I'm afraid I had to go out of town. Nurse Ross and Dr. Sellers are taking care of them…. No, no, they're not sick… Really? Are you sure he'll agree?… That would be wonderful."

The hope in her words buoyed him. This sounded like good news.

"Yes, I'll set things up with Mr. Franco and call you Monday. Absolutely…. Don't be too hard on yourself, Candy. You've been through a lot. And thank you."

She clicked off and stood there, breathing heavily as if she'd just run a marathon. Perhaps, emotionally, she had.

"Well?" Mark asked.

"I can't stand here and talk. I need to move."

"Closet," he said.

"Sorry?"

"Let's suit up and go for a walk." He strode into the bedroom and unlocked a door half-hidden by the large dresser. From inside, he fetched ski caps, gloves, a windbreaker and boots. Good thing he kept a range of sizes available for friends.

Sam had already zipped her jacket when he rejoined her. They bundled up and set out into a landscape dusted with white. A few flakes still scampered through the air, but, as Mark had guessed, a big snowfall didn't appear likely.

"Candy was in a motorcycle accident," Sam said as they crunched their way across the gravel. "She's scraped and bruised but nothing broken."

She'd ridden on a motorcycle less than two weeks after a cesarean? "She could rupture her incision."

"The ER doctor called in an ob-gyn. She's fine but really sore."

Thank goodness she'd escaped major injury. "How did it happen?"

At the edge of the road, they turned and walked side by side along the shoulder. "She was riding behind her new boyfriend, a fellow with the charming name of Spider. And tattoos to match." Between frosty breaths, Sam explained that the bike had barely started rolling forward when it somehow overturned.

Spider, who'd suffered a sprained arm, had blamed Candy for throwing him off balance. "She said he was waving to a friend and showing off."

"Sounds like poor judgment all around." Mark was grateful the tumble hadn't been more serious.

"She kept remembering how he'd wanted to take Colin with them, just held in her arms. Something about teaching the little guy not to be afraid. Can you imagine?"

Unfortunately, he could.

"She's really shook up. You know how kids have this sense of invulnerability? Well, hers got stripped away." Sam kicked a pinecone out of her path. "She said that if I hadn't intervened, she might have agreed. All she could think about as she was lying on the pavement was that she might have killed Colin."

Mark's stomach tensed at the mental picture of that trusting little fellow lost forever. "You said something about setting up a meeting with Tony?"

"She got a text from Jon a few days ago, asking if they can be friends again. She promises to drag him in to sign those relinquishment papers." Sam tugged her cap over her ears. "She swears she's given up any idea of taking the triplets. That it scares her just to think about how un-prepared she is to protect them."

"How can you be sure she won't reconsider?"

"Well, there's always that possibility. But she sounded, well, like she's growing up, changing. I know this isn't a simple process, but I truly don't believe she's going to want them back."

"Then you can stop worrying about that." He rested his hand lightly on the small of her back. "Congratulations."

Her pace took on a new jauntiness. "They're safe! Isn't that wonderful? Now I can focus on gearing up for Christmas. That party's going to be great fun! You are planning to bring your sister, aren't you?"

Ahead, a squirrel darted up a tall tree. "Someone ought to tell that critter he's supposed to hibernate."

"Tree squirrels don't hibernate."

Mark stared at her in mock dismay. "Next you'll tell me bats don't use radar."

"Technically they don't," Sam informed him. "They use something called echolocation."

"What are you, a nature expert?"

She chuckled. "You'd be surprised at the questions kids ask pediatricians. They expect you to be an expert on everything. *Some* of us don't go around ducking questions."

He tried to figure out what she meant. "Excuse me?"

"I asked if you were bringing your sister to the party. You changed the subject."

"I will if she arrives in time." Wryly, he added, "Or if she arrives at all."

"She has to," Sam told him briskly. "I've got space in my cabinet all picked out for that glassware you're going to buy me."

He'd almost forgotten their bet. "While I'd like to get

my kiss under the mistletoe, I hope you're right." Besides, going to a yard sale might be fun. Especially if Sam went with him.

"How exactly do you make a snowball?" she asked sweetly. Too sweetly.

"You're the one who grew up in Seattle. They get more snow than Florida," he answered.

"You're the one who owns a cabin in Big Bear." From a patch where a thin layer had accumulated, she scooped a handful of the white stuff and pressed it like a patty.

"If you throw that at me…"

She tossed it at a tree trunk. "You'll what?"

Spotting another meager drift deeper into the wooded area, Mark beat her there in a couple of strides and snatched up a gloveful of his own. "Return the favor."

"But I didn't!" Sam grabbed his arm.

"Then I guess I'll have to do this." He dropped the snow and gathered her close. On the street, an SUV chugged past, but Mark ignored it as he brushed his lips across Sam's cold cheek until he reached the warmth of her mouth.

Her arms twined around him. Through the thick layers of clothing, he felt her heart thrumming to match his own.

Deliciously isolated in a column of their own heat, he enjoyed the lingering taste of Sam's mouth and the naughty flick of her tongue. As her hands smoothed along the back of his neck, she stood on tiptoe and her hips met his.

Desire arrowed through him. He felt as if the entire woods might burst into snow-defying flame. "Think we can make it home?"

"I don't know," she murmured against his jaw. "Maybe we could just build a snow cave and do it here."

"Impractical."

"Then we should…"

"Go," he finished.

"Fast," she added.

So they did.

Chapter Thirteen

Sam loved the way Mark burst through his usual restraint as he swept her across the cabin and into the bedroom. He tossed his windbreaker onto the floor and, the instant she finished unzipping her jacket, peeled it off, as well.

"Damn boots," he said, flinging aside his ski cap. "Let's leave them on."

Sam shook out her hair. "I don't think that's such a great idea. We might streak mud on the…"

Her protest got lost as he tossed her onto the bed, knelt beside her and smoothed up the pink sweater. The feel of his lips against her breasts sent her reeling.

When he released her, Sam curled around to unbuckle his belt and work open his pants. "You don't play around," Mark said admiringly as he helped her.

"I *do* play around, lucky for you." She basked in the scent of his aftershave lotion and the powerful sight of his chest as he shrugged off his pullover. If she could just get that zipper down… There!

As he rolled her over, her boots clumped to the floor. Muttering impatiently, Mark kicked off his own. "That *is* better."

"And so is this," she said, arching to trace a heated path down Mark's chest with her tongue.

"Incredible." He broke off in a gasp. She had found her way to his erection.

Sam liked feeling this man grow taut beneath her, knowing he was nearing the edge of his control. Then she lifted her head, and Mark seized the initiative. With a few skillful movements, he stripped off her jeans and brought her down, ready for action. Conditioned by years of caution, Sam nearly reminded him that they ought to use protection against pregnancy, until she remembered that she didn't need it anymore.

And she knew she had no need of any other kind of protection with Mark.

Hot longing spread through her as he joined them with long, lustful strokes. Briefly, he paused to brush back her hair and kiss her. Then he filled her again and again, until Sam lost all awareness of anything but him.

At her fevered urging, he drove into her so deeply that she could feel them both melting into a fiery wave. They crested it as one, pleasure leaping and sparking around them like hot lava.

A soft glimmer bathed them in the cool quiet of the room. "Sam," Mark began.

Was he going to say he loved her? She felt a touch afraid, a touch hopeful. Maybe she should say it first. Because she *did* love him.

Sam felt the sting of apprehension. Wonderful things had happened today. To put their feelings into words might tempt fate.

She touched a finger to his lips. "Don't talk."

He nibbled her finger. "Why not?"

Mark wouldn't understand about this silly superstition. "Let's go eat." She wriggled away from him. Shivering in the chill air, she grabbed for her clothes.

"Earlier, you accused *me* of ducking questions. Why can't I talk?" he demanded.

She might as well get this over with. "Because it's bad luck."

"What is?"

Maybe he hadn't meant to say he loved her, or that this was the most special moment of his life, or that they belonged together. Perhaps she'd misread the signs, and he'd been on the verge of suggesting they take up clog dancing.

Sam tossed over his pants. "Get dressed, you stud, and quit quizzing me. I'm hungry."

Aside from a skeptical look, Mark complied without further argument.

Since neither of them felt like cooking, they drove into the town, which early darkness had transformed into a fairyland of Christmas lights. There they discovered a range of cuisines from Italian to Mexican to Chinese, along with mountain-themed names like Lumberjack, Grizzly Manor Café and Himalayan Restaurant. They chose a barbecue place and loaded up on back ribs and fried coconut shrimp.

Being around Mark seemed to involve eating a lot of unhealthy food. Sam couldn't have cared less.

They drove home, lit the gas log in the fireplace, and made love in front of it.

There might be no such thing as perfect happiness, she mused later as she lay in Mark's arms in the loft, with a magnificent A-framed view of pine trees and a brilliantly starry sky. But right now, she couldn't ask for anything more.

ON SUNDAY MORNING, THEY MADE pancakes. Afterward, Mark washed the dishes, while Sam, who'd been reluctant to disturb her friends earlier, put in a call to check on the triplets.

As far as Mark could tell from eavesdropping, everything was all right with the babies. After a lively discussion of their sleep and eating habits, Sam fell silent, listening.

"He did what?" she cried, and grinned. "You're kidding! One night with the triplets and... Which of you changed your mind?"

Hoping he was right, Mark pointed questioningly to his ring finger. Sam nodded.

So the marriage plans were back on. Mark could hardly wait until she clicked off. "Well?"

"They're engaged again," she told him. "Lori swears she isn't going to waste time planning a big ceremony. They don't want to wait."

"But didn't you and Jennifer already buy bridesmaids' dresses? Plus she's got a big family in Colorado." Last fall, Mark had overheard months of chatter about his nurse's elaborate plans for a church wedding followed by a reception.

"She wants a simple ceremony with a few close friends," Sam replied cheerily. "Later, she and Jared will throw a big party."

He finished loading the dishwasher and asked the big question, "Which of them changed their mind about having babies?"

Sam twinkled at him. "You sure you wouldn't rather wait till tomorrow and ask them yourself?"

Mark assumed a bland expression. "You're right. It's no big deal anyway."

"Of course it's a big deal!" she flared. "That's why they broke up."

"Then I guess you ought to tell me."

Sam poured a fresh cup of coffee. "Well…" She took a slow sip, drawing out the tension.

"It must have been Jared," Mark teased, although he suspected the opposite was true. "He's around babies all day. Getting stuck with them at night, too, must have been too much for the man."

"Don't be ridiculous! He didn't feel stuck."

"So it's Lori."

Sam settled onto the couch. "She says Jared's nothing like her father, who refused to get up at night or even change a diaper. And her parents had six kids! That's why her mother dumped so many child-care duties on her."

"And she developed an aversion to motherhood. But Connie, Courtney and Colin fixed her, did they?"

"Those munchkins charmed the socks off her. She asked if she could borrow them now and then. I said yes, of course."

When Mark sat down beside her, Sam nestled against him. He looped an arm around her, careful not to jostle the coffee cup. "After the counseling clinic leaves, we should turn those offices into a wedding chapel. Lori and Jared, Tony and Kate—we've got a full slate of weddings coming up."

Sam's eyes shone. "We could offer a full-service facility. Get married on the premises, conceive in the fertility suite, and deliver right in the same building."

"Dr. Tartikoff's keen on innovation," Mark mused. "He should love it."

"Dr. Tartikoff?" She looked impressed. "I had no idea we were aspiring that high."

"Nothing's firmed up yet," he warned. "In fact, I shouldn't have mentioned it."

Sam sighed. "Don't worry. I've become the soul of discretion."

"How long do you suppose that will last?"

"Two to three hours. Or possibly days. I'm in a beatific frame of mind, what with the Christmas party less than a week away."

At the thought of Christmas, a shadow flitted across Mark's sunlit horizon. He ought to warn Sam that Mrs. Wycliff and her daughter might attend. But if he brought them up now and Sam went nuclear, that would be unfair to Ian, who'd stuck his neck out to invite them.

Besides, no one had confirmed that they planned to be there. Why risk spoiling today's mellow mood?

Instead, he brought up a happier topic. "I spotted a Christmas tree lot on the way up here. We could surprise the triplets."

Sam set her empty cup on the coffee table. "They're too young to be surprised."

"No one's too young to be surprised," Mark assured her. "Birth comes as a big surprise to newborns, believe me."

"It comes as a shock," she corrected. "You can only be surprised if you're expecting things to be a certain way in the first place. Babies don't have a fixed sense of how things are supposed to be until roughly 18 months."

He regarded her in amusement. "I should know better than to argue about child development with a pediatrician."

"By the way, I'd love to get a Christmas tree." She extended her legs across his, half sitting in his lap. "We don't have to leave yet, do we?"

"No. I have a much better idea of what we could do this morning," he told her.

As it turned out, so did she.

FROM THE TOP OF AN OVERSTUFFED closet in her house, Sam retrieved a box of ornaments she'd collected, by chance and by luck, over the years. Rainbow glass globes and glittery stars, shimmering angels, cherub dolls, along with velvet bows and strings of lights. Some had been gifts, others yard-sale finds or impulse buys at post-holiday clearance sales.

Despite their admitted mutual ignorance of tree trimming, she and Mark managed—with advice from the internet—to wedge the tree into a base, fill it with water and prop it upright. Then they hung and dangled ornaments and lights around the aromatic branches. For good measure, they also tacked a strand of colored lights across the front of the house.

The triplets, who'd been fussy in the car, had calmed once Sam got them home. True, their feedings and diaper changes slowed the tree decorating, but she enjoyed the sense that they'd already begun to feel at home here.

The little innocents hadn't a clue that they'd already worked a Christmas miracle, Sam mused as she stood atop the ladder, capping the tree with a giant star. When she and Mark had arrived at Jared's to pick up the babies, Lori had beamed at her fiancé, who'd scarcely stopped touching her while they regaled their two friends with their plans to get married as soon as next week.

Lori still wanted Sam and Jen to be her bridesmaids, and there'd be a small reception immediately following the ceremony. Her list of a few close friends was expanding to include coworkers, and just before Sam left, Lori had mentioned that she would invite her family, after all.

"I don't want to hurt their feelings," she'd said. "I mean, I only plan to get married once."

Tearing her thoughts back to the present, Sam descended the ladder. Mark gripped her protectively around the waist and lifted her from the last step to slide her down the length of his body.

"I like the way that feels." She draped her arms over his shoulders. "Think anyone would notice if we made the most of it?"

Clearing his throat, Mark dipped his head toward their audience arrayed in carriers around the tree. "Let's keep this G-rated."

"They're too young to tell the difference."

"Science is always discovering unsuspected aspects to memory," he murmured. "Do you want them to end up on a psychiatrist's couch forty years from now, explaining why they have strange fantasies involving Christmas trees?"

Sam poked him in the ribs. "All right, then. Stand back."

He complied. She turned off the overheads, then switched on the tiny lights.

The tree glowed with a display of treasures transformed into fairy gifts. Outside, twilight had fallen, which only intensified the brilliance inside. One of the babies cooed appreciatively. If it was a burp, Sam didn't want to know it.

"Their first Christmas tree," she said. "Mine, too."

"You mean in this house?"

"Since I've been an adult," she clarified. "How about you?"

Courtney began to cry. Without missing a beat, Mark picked her up. "In Florida, my staff gave me a miniature tree that sat on my coffee table. Does that count?"

"No," she said.

"Then it's the first."

"We're virgins."

"I wouldn't put it that way."

Sam basked in the warmth of his gaze. Who could have imagined two weeks ago that today she'd feel so free and lighthearted?

Must be the spirit of Christmas. And, she conceded as she stole a glance sideways in the dimness, it was because of Mark.

He seemed easy and natural around her and the babies. There was, she supposed, a reserve in him that might always be there, but she'd never wanted the sort of relationship where a couple did everything in lockstep. He could live in his house and keep his schedule, and they could be together when it suited them both.

Things were just fine.

THE WEEK BEFORE CHRISTMAS always passed a bit slowly at the hospital. Patients avoided elective surgeries and the number of births dropped off slightly. As much as possible, doctors scheduled C-sections before or after the holiday period, when many of them went out of town.

As a result, Mark had the treat of performing extra deliveries. Holding each newborn felt even more special than usual, because of the triplets. This little boy showed a trace of Colin's spunk. That girl appeared worried, like Courtney. And when a small defect presented itself, like Connie's discoloration, he could assure the parents from the heart that they would fall in love with the baby just as deeply.

On Wednesday, Dr. Tartikoff called to discuss ideas for adding fertility center staff and to ask about the timetable for renovating the facilities. Although he hadn't officially committed, he promised to make a decision soon after the first of the year.

Informed by phone, Chandra was ecstatic. "Keep him happy, Mark, whatever it takes."

"Within reason." He wasn't sure how much to believe of Owen's reputation for being difficult. So far, Mark had seen no signs of temperament, but then, he hadn't crossed the man, either.

"The board is counting on you to land him," the vice president said. "Don't let us down."

"I'll do my best. Merry Christmas." Mark hoped she didn't detect a note of irony.

"Yes, yes, of course. Merry Christmas."

Chandra had once mentioned having two grandchildren. He hoped that when they jumped onto her lap, they didn't get frostbite on their little rear ends.

On Thursday afternoon, Jennifer stopped into Mark's office to confirm that Mrs. Wycliff and her daughter would be dropping by the party. "She's a real dynamo," the PR director told him. "Honestly, Sam's met her match. Or rather, she *will* be meeting her match."

"Let's hope they hit it off." Mark felt a moment of disquiet. But surely Eleanor's involvement was the best Christmas present the clinic could receive.

"Samantha's been happier this week than I've ever seen her," Jennifer added. "You're good for her."

Obviously, Sam's closest friends knew of the weekend excursion, but Mark felt obliged to sound a note of caution. "I'd rather this didn't become a topic of general discussion."

"It won't."

"Thanks."

"Ready for tomorrow night?" Jennifer asked.

He had nothing scheduled Christmas Eve except on-call duty. "What do you mean?"

"You haven't forgotten our annual caroling?" she chided.

"Actually, I did." Members of the senior staff traditionally sang carols throughout the hospital to cheer up those who had to work as well as patients stuck here when they wanted to be home. "Thanks for reminding me."

"I'll drop the lyric sheets on your desk," Jennifer said. "Seven o'clock. We'll start on the top floor and work our way down."

"Great." He *did* enjoy the tradition. Last year, Samantha had displayed a throaty contralto that struck Mark as incredibly sexy.

After Jennifer left, he checked his email and clicked open an angel-bedecked card from his sister. It included the notation, "See you around three o'clock Saturday."

He emailed back directions to the hospital, details of the party and a reminder of his cell phone number. "I can't wait to see how you're doing."

Bryn was really coming. She'd be keeping her word, at last. This year, he felt certain—almost—that if he were a fortune-teller, he'd see a yard sale and a glass knickknack in his future.

This was one bet he looked forward to losing.

Chapter Fourteen

On Christmas Eve, after eating a quick dinner at home, Sam took the babies to the hospital nursery. With plenty of cribs available on the holiday, the staff had volunteered to babysit for the carolers.

Jennifer's Rosalie was already here, along with Tara, Tony's month-old daughter. Tiny as they were, each baby already had quite a story, Sam mused. Rosalie and the triplets had been relinquished, while Tara had been born to a surrogate mother. At least, Kate had started out as a surrogate. After Tony's wife, Esther, also an attorney, abandoned him and their unborn baby for a high-powered job in Washington, he'd stepped in as Kate's birthing partner. By Thanksgiving Day, when Tara arrived, the couple had fallen in love. They planned to marry in the spring, as soon as his divorce became final, and Kate now volunteered at the clinic as a peer counselor.

Lingering beside Connie's bassinet, Sam tried to imagine what it would be like to be a bride walking down an aisle. As a teenager, with the threat of cancer hanging over her head, she'd never dared fantasize about her wedding. Later, she'd figured she would rather spend her money on a good cause than a fancy ceremony. Now, she had to admit she'd love to indulge just a little. Beautiful flowers filling a chapel, a couple of friends in elegant dresses, and, most important, a man waiting for her by the altar, his face suffused with love.

Wonder who that could be....

"Dr. Forrest?" A nurse signaled for her attention. "There's a woman in the hall asking for you."

"About the caroling?"

The nurse frowned. "I don't think so."

Sam shifted into take-charge mode. "Thanks. I'll handle it." Who could this be on Christmas Eve?

In the nearly deserted third-floor corridor, a stocky woman with disheveled graying hair stood, arms folded. From her wrinkled housedress to her truculent expression, she inspired immediate wariness. But Sam strove not to judge by appearances.

"I'm Dr. Forrest. What can I do for you?" She dispensed with the usual holiday greetings, since this woman didn't appear to be in the mood.

"I'm Vivien Babcock. I'd like to know why there's nobody at the counseling clinic. You must all be too busy planning your big party tomorrow to waste time on actual clients." The woman's jaw thrust forward.

Sam fought down her instinctive dislike of an exaggerated sense of entitlement. Experience had taught that sometimes the most disagreeable people were the most in need of help. "Is this an emergency?" *It had better be, on Christmas Eve.*

Vivien continued to glare. "I've decided to leave my husband. He's a rotten piece of scum."

Sam scrutinized the woman for signs of abuse. She detected no obvious bruises and no wincing or favoring an arm or leg that might be injured. "You're leaving him tonight?"

"That's right—you know how they always get ugly on holidays" was the vague reply.

Upstairs, the carolers must be wondering what had delayed Sam. Straining for patience, she asked, "Who are 'they'?"

"Men," Vivien snapped. "He's my third husband, so I guess I'm an expert."

An abusive husband *was* likely to use force to prevent his wife from leaving. "I can arrange to admit you to a women's shelter."

"Is that all?" Her lip curled.

"If you feel in danger, you should ask the police to accompany you, or simply leave without telling him," Sam advised. "Walk away from the hospital and don't go home again. Are there children who might be in harm's way?"

"My kids are grown, and a fat lot they care what happens to me. Is that all you have to say?" Vivien's voice rose, with no apparent concern for the open doors to patient rooms along the hall.

"I run a small counseling clinic, not a crisis center," Sam told her. "However, I'd be happy to put in a call to—"

"Never mind." With a toss of her unbrushed hair, the woman marched off. Not limping, Sam noted.

Perhaps she should hurry after her, try to learn the whole story and figure out what resources she needed. Sam hated turning away a person who was clearly in pain and possibly in danger, no matter how obnoxious she might be. But tonight, she lacked both the energy and the will to pursue the matter.

After that wondrously relaxing getaway with Mark, she'd had a busy week. On Monday, the triplets' father had gladly signed papers giving up his rights. Although Candy still had roughly three weeks before signing her final relinquishment, she'd admitted to feeling relief at being free again.

"My aunt in Colorado invited me to move in with her,"

the young woman had told Sam. "She's a hairdresser and she's going to help me get into cosmetology school. It'll be fun."

"You sure you're okay with this?" Sam had pressed, despite her anguish at the possibility that Candy might renege.

"If I gave them to someone else, I'd probably worry," Candy had said. "But it's you, Sam. In a funny way, I always kind of felt like you were their mother."

"I guess I did, too."

While the situation with the babies seemed on track, the clinic's immediate future still hung in the balance. Several volunteers had suggested possible new locations, but despite Sam's inquiries, none had panned out. Then a salsa band canceled its promise to play for free at the fundraiser. Luckily, she was able to replace it with a mariachi band. She already knew some of the musicians, who were related to a twelve-year-old brain cancer survivor, a onetime patient of Sam's whom she'd referred to Children's Hospital, a few miles away in the city of Orange. According to the last report she'd received, his cancer was in remission.

Another battle won, at least temporarily.

On the top floor, she emerged from the elevator and followed the strains of "We Three Kings" around a corner. There stood a hardy and mostly on-key band: Jared and Lori, on whose finger sparkled a ring; Tony and Kate with her five-year-old son, who kept muffing the words; Jennifer and Ian, nursing director Betsy Raditch, PR assistant Willa Lightner and her teenage son and daughter. And, overshadowing them all, Mark. His gaze lit instantly on Sam as if he'd been watching for her.

Happiness tingled through her. As the carolers launched into "Joy to the World," Sam moved to his side and united her voice with his.

On Christmas morning, Mark awoke in a bed that wasn't his. Today, however, he felt very much at home in it.

Last night, after caroling, he'd helped Sam strap the babies into the van and then followed them home in his car. They'd lit the tree and let the enchantment ripple through them.

Since they had busy schedules for Christmas Day, they'd exchanged gifts that evening. He'd bought her a quilt hand-made by hospital volunteers, with panels that reproduced children's colorful drawings. She'd given him a home golf simulator that allowed him to practice his swing and get it analyzed by computer. Sure to improve his golf game, and possibly his mood.

Then they'd made love and gone to sleep in each other's arms.

During the night, they'd taken turns getting up for feedings, since Sam had refused to ask a nurse to work on a holiday night. Mark didn't mind. Sitting in the quiet hours holding the infants, he'd stumbled into a magical connection with them.

Unbelievable, that such tiny bundles could hold an entire future. As he gazed down at their faces, he saw the future unfolding: toddlers learning to walk, children reading words aloud, teenagers holding hands with a first love or rushing to share the results of a college application. The tears and disappointments, the challenges and triumphs. All this, and they still fit into the crook of his arm.

In the morning, he slept later than usual to compensate for his night duty. Samantha slumbered deeply beside him. Good, she needed it.

As he rose, she shifted to sprawl diagonally across the double bed. Eyes closed, breathing regular, blond hair riot-ing around her…she might have been the picture of beauty, save for her light snoring. Actually, Mark decided, she was still the picture of beauty, with sound effects.

He'd received only one call from the hospital last night, about a patient in the early stages of labor. Mark had monitored her progress during feedings, and, after dressing and eating breakfast, arrived at the maternity ward in time for the delivery.

A beautiful little boy. The large Italian family that gathered to welcome him showered Mark with thanks, holiday greetings and homemade cookies.

That morning, he ushered three more babies into the world, including one by C-section. As always, Mark was grateful to be part of such miracles.

But, for a change, he was also a little impatient to get back to the miracles that had come into his own life.

SAM HAD A GREAT FEELING about this party. Although she'd wondered whether having it on Christmas Day might discourage volunteers, several came early to finish decorating the suite with paper flowers, a piñata and holiday lights, and more showed up just before the two o'clock start time. The caterer arrived with boxes of hot hors d'oeuvres, while the initial trickle of guests swelled to a torrent, many with checks to contribute. Ian had offered to keep track of those, and drop them off at the bank's night deposit box.

A volunteer Santa distributed small gifts to children, joking with them about his red-trimmed white sombrero. As for the band, its music set people's toes tapping and hips wiggling.

While the actual event hadn't drawn a lot of interest from the press, reporter Tom LaGrange had stopped by with a photographer. Jennifer, who was discreetly steering him around, had presented him with a new brochure about the clinic's plans. Optimistic plans, Sam had to admit, considering what a large amount they'd need now that they could no longer use the hospital's facilities.

They'd taken for granted not only this suite, but free access to utilities and the internet. She'd also grown accustomed to dropping in here between other duties. That would be difficult when she had to drive to another location.

Sam gave herself a mental shake. This was no occasion for negativity. Her friends and volunteers were laughing and enjoying the alcohol-free punch, and Mark...she kept having to force her gaze away from him as he joked with the appreciative crowd around him.

Were her feelings written as plainly on her face as she feared? It was too soon to let the hospital grapevine get hold of their relationship. Sam wasn't certain yet what kind of relationship they had, except that he'd become so entwined in her thoughts and daydreams that she could scarcely believe only weeks ago they'd been nothing more than verbal sparring partners.

Then, with a jolt, she spotted a boy seated on a folding chair near the band, shaking a castanet in synch with the music. The rest of the room faded, leaving only this youngster. He was small for his twelve years, his face was puffy from steroids, and his tasseled Santa hat had slipped back to reveal a bald head.

No one had told her Artie Ortega's cancer was back.

Mischievous and smart, Artie had recovered from his initial brain tumor. Obviously, it had returned and was being treated aggressively.

Tamping down her concern, Sam pasted a smile on her face and hurried over. "I didn't realize you'd joined the band." She gestured toward his castanet.

"You didn't know I was a rock star?" he shot back.

Sam slid into the chair beside him. "So how's it going?"

"I met a cute girl at a party last night." Doffing the hat, he ducked his head to show the words "Luv, Mellie" scrawled in black marker. "I think she likes me."

"How could she help it?" Sam teased.

Artie's mother, a rotund woman who smelled of cinnamon, perched in the chair on his far side. "He's beating this, Dr. Sam."

"I can see that." She couldn't really, but Sam hoped it was true. If she'd won her battle with cancer, why not Artie?

The pair filled her in on the latest developments in the boy's life. His older sister had had a baby, elevating him to the rank of uncle. His father, laid off from his job, had recently found work again. Good news, all of it.

As the conversation wound down, Mrs. Ortega stared across the room. "Who's that? I think I've seen her on the news." She indicated a tall, patrician woman talking intently with Ian.

"No, who's *that?*" Artie indicated a teenage girl standing with the new arrival. Unlike her mother—Sam presumed they were related, given their similar heights and nutmeg-brown hair—the girl had an open, friendly face. A very pretty face, as the boy had obviously noticed.

"Someone I haven't met yet," Sam informed him. "She looks a tad old for you."

"I'm a man of the world," Artie informed her loftily.

She gave him a hug. "You certainly are."

As soon as she released him, he pulled his hat on, covering the other girl's signature. "Don't want her to think I'm taken."

"Why, you flirt!" Sam joked. "You're going to leave a trail of broken hearts."

Sadness flickered across his young face. "Girls just pretend to flirt with me. I don't look so good right now." His smile returned. "But that'll be over soon."

"Go for it, champ." Reluctantly, Sam excused herself to return to her duties. Mark had joined the group around the tall woman and her daughter, and judging by his serious manner, they weren't merely discussing the punch.

She'd better go find out what that was all about.

FOR THE FIRST HOUR OF THE PARTY, Mark had been swept up by the Hot and Happy Christmas spirit. But while he realized that three o'clock was merely an estimate for his sister's arrival, he'd begun checking his watch instinctively since that hour passed.

When he dialed Bryn's cell phone number, it went through to voice mail. That made sense, since she shouldn't be gabbing on the phone while driving, but he wished he could reach her.

Where was she now on her journey from Phoenix? Surely she'd crossed the state line into California. Possibly she was entering Orange County's northern limits right now, a mere half hour's drive from Safe Harbor.

He wondered how much she'd changed in the past five years. She must be thirty-three, and she'd lived those years hard. Yet to see her healthy and in control of her life would more than compensate for a few added wrinkles and gray hairs, and for the nights he'd spent searching for her in bars and alcohol-drenched flophouses.

But what about the lies, the money he'd wasted on rehab, the sense of angry frustration, and the silence after she disappeared?

Thou shalt not hold grudges. Thou shalt be grateful

for the prodigal's return. Except, a tiny voice kept asking, what if she didn't come? What if, once again, she went back on her word?

He pushed those concerns aside when Ian introduced him to Mrs. Wycliff and her daughter. Both were charming, and filled with ideas. Eleanor, as she insisted everyone call her, had already talked to a number of influential friends. "They agree that this sounds like a worthwhile project. True, there are a number of programs asking for money, but how exciting to build something practically from the ground up."

"It's special because it's named after that baby who died," added Libby Wycliff, her eyes bright with tears.

"Don't start crying now!" her mother said. "It's Christmas."

"I won't." The girl bit down on a trembling lip. It was only a few months since her father's death, Mark remembered. Libby must be transferring some of her emotions to this new project.

"I suppose I shouldn't have jumped the gun, but I called the city of Safe Harbor's human services coordinator, and guess what?" Eleanor told him. "She's been trying to figure out how to expand the family and teen offerings at their community center. When she heard this was Dr. Forrest's clinic, she got all excited. We may have a new home already!"

"That's terrific," Ian said.

A new home. It *sounded* great, but Sam already knew the human services coordinator. Why hadn't they discussed this possibility?

"Did I hear my name?" Sam joined them, her cheerful expression a touch strained. A short while ago, he'd seen her talking to a little boy who was obviously a cancer patient.

As Ian made introductions, Mark wished he'd informed her sooner about Eleanor's interest. For one thing, he didn't want to add to Sam's concerns right now. Also, he'd assumed Ian's friend would show up here as an interested newcomer, nothing more. Instead, she'd apparently appointed herself to represent the counseling center to the city.

He checked his watch. Nearly three-thirty. It was just as well Bryn had been delayed, he supposed; he'd hate for her to walk into the middle of a tense situation.

He glanced at Sam. She didn't seem to take offense. Instead, she listened politely, if guardedly, to Eleanor's explanation of what she'd been doing and how excited she was about the plans. It must be the Christmas spirit. Or was it possible that, as the mother of three, she finally felt ready to hand over the clinic to someone else?

SAM RESTRAINED AN URGE to poke Mark in the side for failing to warn her about this eager-beaver socialite. Still, the clinic had to move within the next few weeks, and it could use a sponsor. Also, when Jennifer mentioned Ian's wealthy contact, Sam had put her off—and never brought up the subject again. No wonder her friends had decided to act independently.

Still, Eleanor Wycliff's imperious manner was likely to intimidate the very people who most needed counseling. Also, from the way she talked about her friends' fundraising balls, Sam doubted they had any real concept of how this low-key, grassroots project operated.

As for coming under the city's sponsorship, Sam had been putting off any discussion of that possibility as a last resort. "Once you get officials involved, there's always red tape," she explained to Eleanor after they'd chatted for a while. "What's special about the Edward Serra Clinic is that teenagers and women can just wander in and talk to a peer counselor, or a doctor, like me. They don't have to fill out a bunch of paperwork first."

Eleanor dismissed the notion with a lift of her elegant shoulders. "I'm sure we can work around that."

"This will be so much fun," added Libby, a sweet girl with an air of fragility. "My best friend's going to collect baby stuff for the clients at her next birthday party, instead of gifts. Isn't that cool?"

"That's very generous." Sam liked the daughter, and she supposed she would like the mother, too, once she got to know Eleanor better.

It *was* a relief to think of sharing responsibility for the clinic. Not that Sam intended to abandon her vision, but recently it had begun to feel more like a burden and less like the realization of a dream.

More playtime with the triplets. More leisurely evenings with Mark, and mornings waking up to his warmth lingering on the sheets. She craved those things, and she deserved them.

"Sam, I think you're needed." Ian nodded toward Jennifer, who was standing across the room with Tom LaGrange and several other people. The photographer's flash went off, and Tom was taking rapid notes as he talked to someone Sam couldn't see.

Jennifer's anxious gaze caught Sam's. Something was wrong. "I'll go see what the problem is." She excused herself and crossed the room. Unexpectedly, Eleanor broke away and walked with her.

At Sam's suggestion that she didn't have to get involved, the socialite replied, "This is a fundraiser for *our* clinic. I'm already involved."

Too late to argue. Besides, at that moment Sam caught

sight of the woman who'd been hidden from view. It was Vivien Babcock, her hair even more matted than yesterday, her face flushed and her voice painfully loud.

Whatever she might be saying, the reporter was eating up every word.

Chapter Fifteen

"What a sham this whole thing is!" Vivien proclaimed in slurred tones as Sam and Eleanor approached. "A bunch of fancy people making themselves feel important. You should see the way they treated me!"

"Who *is* that creature?" Eleanor murmured.

"A very troubled woman," Sam answered. "Let's find out exactly what she wants." Despite her irritation, she hadn't forgotten Vivien's declaration that she planned to leave her husband. That was one of those turning points when people's lives could explode, or implode.

"Is she a client?" Eleanor asked.

"She dropped in last night. Christmas Eve, after dinner. Got mad that nobody was staffing the clinic." After this quiet aside, Sam moved to join the group around Jennifer. "Hello, Mrs. Babcock."

Vivien's jaw tightened pugnaciously. "Well! Here's the great doctor who gave me the brush-off last night."

"I tried to refer you to a more appropriate, full-service facility," Sam said calmly. "You chose to leave."

"Well, you didn't try hard enough." With a glittering, almost triumphant look, Vivien peeled back her blouse, exposing a massive black-and-blue patch across her shoulder and chest. With only the bra protecting her from indecency, she turned to display welts across her back. Gasps went up from the observers. The camera was flashing again, and several onlookers raised cell phones to take pictures. "This is what my husband did when I told him I was leaving. You could have prevented this."

No, you could have prevented it. "I advised you to call the police, or simply leave without telling him."

"Easy for you to say!"

Mark was heading in their direction, his face creased with concern. To the reporter, Sam explained, "No one threw anybody out. The Edward Serra Clinic offers informal counseling. We don't have a professional staff yet. I offered to arrange for Mrs. Babcock to enter a women's shelter, and I'll do that now. First, though, we have to report this to the police. Unless you've already filed a report?" She raised an eyebrow at the woman.

Vivien's face crumpled. "My husband *is* a cop."

Sam's stomach tensed. No wonder the woman felt powerless and filled with rage. True, she had unreasonable expectations of the clinic, along with a harsh and not very likable personality, but she was clearly hurting inside and out. "Then I can understand…"

"Oh, you can understand?" Vivien mocked. "Sure you can."

"You're drunk. Drunk and selfish." Eleanor's voice snapped through the air like a whip. "Dr. Forrest offered to help you last night and you threw it in her face. You brought this on yourself."

"How dare you!" Vivien tensed, as if she'd like to land a few blows on this elegant woman, a startling contrast to her own sagging, pouchy self. Both of them were in their late forties, Sam estimated, but what a difference.

"People are giving up their Christmases to help women like you," Eleanor told the interloper. "Of course that man had no right to beat you, but you should get a lawyer and make him pay for it."

"Easy for you to say. Get a lawyer! As if they grew on trees. Maybe for rich people like you."

To short-circuit the argument, Sam caught Vivien's arm. Too late, she realized her mistake. Although it was impossible to see through the sleeve, there must have been a nasty bruise underneath, because the woman let out a yelp.

"I'm sorry." Too late.

"You're both hypocrites!" Vivien cried. "You don't care about the poor or the downtrodden. All you care about is prancing around acting important."

More shutters clicked. Tom held up his recorder, capturing every word.

Barely bothering to yank her blouse into place, Vivien stalked off. "Oh, let her go," Eleanor said. "That woman's beyond saving."

"Nobody's beyond saving!" Sam flared. "If that's the way you think, this is the wrong place for you."

Then she ran to catch up with Vivien Babcock.

MARK, WHO'D BEEN LISTENING from a distance, assessed the situation rapidly. One wealthy donor about to flounce out of the party, deeply offended. A newspaper reporter barely suppressing his glee over stumbling across a controversy. Guests talking and texting on their cell phones, probably sending video around the world.

And then there was Sam disappearing in the wake of an injured woman.

Mark went after Sam.

He found her by the elevators with Vivien Babcock, who had tears streaming down her face. All the anger seemed to have whooshed out of her, leaving her deflated and frightened. "I'm calling someone I know at a shelter," Sam told him. "We have to get her to a safe place and figure out how to handle the situation with the police."

"I'll call the chief at home." Mark occasionally played golf with the man. "The boys in blue may tend to stick together, but once I explain it, I'm sure the chief will take this situation seriously."

"What if he fires my husband?" Vivien cried. "He'll lose his income and his pension. I'll have nothing."

"You'll have nothing if he kills you," Sam replied. The woman fell silent.

Sam's gaze met Mark's. Clearly, she wasn't any more thrilled than he was about having to deal with this situation on Christmas, but when you were a doctor, emergencies came with the territory.

Fifteen minutes later, Mark had talked to the chief and been assured that the officer in question would be immediately suspended, and a report taken by a female officer. Sam's friend from the women's shelter was on her way, and the last hint of fight had gone out of Vivien.

Leaving the pair in the lobby to wait for Sam's friend, Mark returned to the party, or rather to the office suite, since by now the event had officially ended. The mariachi band had departed, the guests were gone, and the caterer was packing away what remained of the food.

Jennifer and Ian were taking down the decorations. "What happened after I left?" Mark asked.

The PR director regarded him glumly. "Mrs. Wycliff left in a huff. She's furious about the whole scene. Libby was in tears over the woman's bruises."

"Eleanor was right," Ian added. "Vivien had no business barging in here roaring drunk, blaming everyone else for her problems."

Unfortunately, that was exactly what alcoholics did, in Mark's experience. They disappointed, disrupted and discarded others. Take Bryn. She was more than an hour overdue, yet she hadn't called. Maybe she was lying somewhere badly injured in a car crash, or maybe she'd just stopped at a bar for liquid fortification.

He should have insisted on buying her a plane ticket, or gone to Phoenix to meet her. Above all, he should have trusted his gut instinct that she hadn't fundamentally changed.

Nobody's beyond saving. Sam's words rang in his ears. But while he admired her generous spirit, and had done what he could to ensure Mrs. Babcock's safety, today he wasn't sure he shared that optimism. About her client *or* his sister.

"Should I call Mrs. Wycliff and apologize on behalf of the hospital administration?" he asked. "This happened under our roof, and the clinic can't afford to lose her."

"I'll call her," Ian said. "I'm sure an apology from you wouldn't hurt, either. But Sam's the real sticking point."

Jennifer folded her arms. "Sam's heart may be in the right place, but this clinic doesn't belong to her. It's named after *my* son, and it's going to fall apart without someone like Eleanor at the helm."

"Good luck persuading Sam of that. She thinks she can carry the entire world on her shoulders," Mark reflected ruefully.

"Well, she can't," Jennifer said. "She made her choice when she adopted the triplets. Her first duty is to them now. She'll be mad at all of us for a while, but if it's a choice between her and Eleanor, we have to cut Sam out of the picture."

Reluctantly, Mark agreed.

BY THE TIME SHE PULLED INTO her driveway that night,
Sam was bone-weary and fed up. Why couldn't other
people get their acts together? Eventually, Vivien had qui-
eted down, but she hadn't expressed any appreciation for
being taken to a safe place or receiving a promise from Dr.
Kendall, whom Sam had also called, to stop by the shelter
and examine her injuries. The only positive note was Sam's
hope that Vivien had bottomed out and would finally get
treatment for her drinking. But what was Eleanor's excuse
for *her* behavior?

The socialite had had no business confronting a client
or making judgment calls. Her job was to raise funds, not
run the clinic. But apparently she felt capable of doing
everything.

Sam had been thrilled at the prospect of relinquish-
ing her responsibilities. Now Eleanor Wycliff's arrogance
made that impossible.

"Does she have to be such a snob?" she asked Connie
as she fumbled with the straps on the baby's car seat.

In the seat behind her sister, Courtney began to whine.
Colin was fussing, too. They must be hungry.

Sam tried to focus on one step at a time. She had to
take them out of the van and into the house before she
could heat their formula and get it into their tiny stomachs.
While the day care center and the occasional night nurse
were a big help, they weren't enough. She loved the triplets
and had been confident that she could handle anything,
yet she'd underestimated the sheer physical challenge of
dealing with three infants. She needed to hire a nanny, a
helper she could rely on day in and day out.

And she needed Mark, his quiet strength supporting her,
his tenderness banishing her worries. He'd stood by her
tonight, even though, as administrator, he probably should
have stayed to placate Mrs. Wycliff. In the past, Sam hadn't

minded making trouble for him, because she'd figured he deserved it. Funny how differently things appeared these days.

As she lifted the little girl, headlights prowled along the quiet street, past houses twinkling with Christmas lights. Her spirits lifted. Had he come to spend the evening with her?

At the curb, a van halted, and she spotted the logo of a TV station on the side. *Oh, just go away!*

"Shall we make a run for it?" she asked Connie. But she couldn't, because Courtney and Colin still had to be carried inside. Besides, the press never seemed to take a hint. They'd knock and phone and make pests of themselves.

Steeling her will, Sam turned to face the news crew. With luck, she could fob them off with a few shots of the triplets. Or, if they'd heard about Vivien Babcock, she'd update them on the situation.

One small counseling clinic was hardly a big story, even on the year's slowest news day.

MARK SETTLED ON HIS SOFA—which was much too hard for comfort, he had to admit—and clicked on the TV. Nothing calmed a man's brain like channel surfing, so he flipped through station after station. Every one seemed to be running a movie about Santa Claus, the nativity or angels, with a liberal sprinkling of ads for after-Christmas sales.

He wondered what Sam was doing. Taking care of the babies, no doubt. Given her reluctance to force a nurse to work on a holiday, she'd be handling the situation alone.

The scent of baby powder. The warm softness of infant skin as he changed a diaper. The tiny burp as he patted a triplet on the back. And, later, Sam's legs tangling with his, her hungry mouth seeking him...

He ached to go over there. But, inevitably, the subject of

Eleanor would come up, and he'd have to admit that he'd spoken to her at length on the phone. And that, basically, he'd given her full control over the clinic.

Once he soothed hurt feelings and explained that the hospital administration was behind her, Eleanor had agreed to stay involved. But there were conditions he'd been in no position to refuse. After today's blowup, Chandra would no doubt insist the clinic vacate the premises immediately. Hard as Sam worked, she hadn't put together a new home *or* a funding plan.

As he tapped the channel-up button, a painfully familiar, blurred image filled the screen: Vivien Babcock stomping away at the Christmas party, her blouse fluttering out behind her. The image shifted, and there was Eleanor, snapping, "Oh, let her go! That woman's beyond saving."

Then Sam, furious, retorted that no one was beyond saving, and that Eleanor didn't belong there. The sound quality was lousy. Unfortunately, not lousy enough to obscure the words.

"Is this cell-phone video an example of the Christmas spirit, Safe Harbor style?" a newswoman commented gleefully from behind the anchor desk of a TV studio. She briefly recapped the spat as if it were some sort of spectator sport. "Now here's an update."

The screen displayed a photograph of Eleanor. In a staticky recording apparently made over the phone, her patrician voice proclaimed, "I have the assurance of Dr. Mark Rayburn that the hospital is behind me one hundred percent. From now on, Dr. Samantha Forrest no longer has any affiliation with the Serra clinic."

Mark sank back and closed his eyes, wishing he could make this whole business disappear. In his entire career, he'd never had to deal with as much bad publicity as Safe

Harbor had suffered in the past four months. First, the misunderstanding about the Safe Haven law had led to multiple baby surrenders, then the press had seized on Sam's silly remarks about beauty makeovers, and now this ridiculous controversy.

Was it him? Was it Sam? Had the medical center inadvertently offended the gods of yellow journalism? He supposed that once the press decided Safe Harbor was newsworthy, any event there got blown out of proportion.

He muted the sound, took out his phone and dialed Sam's number. Mark had no idea if she'd heard the news. If not, he ought to be the one to break it to her. The clinic had been her idea from the start. She'd proposed it, championed it and worked her tail off to make it a reality. She deserved better than to be ousted in a backroom coup, and to learn about it from TV.

Voice mail. Drat!

He sat there fuming. Then, on screen, he saw Sam standing in her driveway, rocking a baby. Looked like Connie, although from this angle he couldn't be sure.

He unmuted the TV. "I've been removed from any role in the clinic's future?" she demanded. "You're sure?"

His heart sank.

The camera shifted to newsman Hayden O'Donnell, his collar raised against the cold. "I'm afraid so. What's your reaction, Dr. Forrest?"

Tensely, she said, "I hope Mrs. Wycliff can put the clinic on solid financial footing." That showed admirable restraint, in Mark's opinion.

"Does the hospital administration have the right to do this?" O'Donnell prodded. "Why do you suppose they kicked the clinic out of its offices in the first place?"

"To make room for their new fertility center, so they can bring in big guns like Dr. Owen Tartikoff." Mark stopped breathing. On the screen, Sam quickly amended, "I mean, someone *like* Dr. Tartikoff."

There was no dissuading the reporter. "Is this true? Dr. Owen Tartikoff is going to head the new fertility center at Safe Harbor?" As Sam remained painfully silent, he addressed the camera. "I think we just got some inside information here, folks. You'll recall that Dr. Tartikoff pioneered a procedure that resulted in the birth of twins to sixty-year-old Olympic gold medalist..."

He went on talking, but Mark didn't hear another word. He'd carelessly told Sam about Dr. Tartikoff. Pillow talk, that was the term. Now, between them, they'd made a huge mess.

A mess so big he wasn't sure he'd be able to clean it up.

Chapter Sixteen

"I can't imagine that they'll fire you." Lori turned gracefully, her silver wedding gown swishing around her. Open boxes tumbled about her apartment living room, some half-filled in preparation for moving to Jared's house and others displaying gifts. Sam wasn't sure which were Christmas presents and which were for the wedding. Not that it mattered. "Have I lost weight? This feels loose."

"You haven't been eating much the past few months," Sam pointed out, kneeling to check the hem. "Pining away for your lost love. This hangs fine, though. You don't need a tailor unless you're *really* picky."

It felt like forever since September, when they'd shopped together for a gown and dresses. And tasted cakes, and hired a photographer. After the engagement ended, Lori had held on to her dress, which proved fortunate, because she was getting married on short notice.

Sam still fit into her silver-and-blue bridesmaid's dress, and she guessed that Jennifer's probably fit, too. The PR director hadn't been available today, Lori said.

Probably hiding from Sam's temper. Or hanging on to a temper of her own, given that yesterday Sam had likely ruined the hospital's chances of landing the great Dr. Tartikoff.

"I just hope I didn't get Mark into trouble," she said as she straightened. "I feel awful."

"Have you talked to him?" Holding back a hank of reddish-brown hair, Lori leaned over the portable playpen.

"I'm afraid to."

"He hasn't called?"

"Or stopped by, either." Sam shivered. Upset as she'd been, she'd never meant to do anything so destructive. "I emailed him an apology."

"Email? Coward!"

"I texted one, too."

"Just as bad!" Lori eyed the babies. "Hey, I have an idea. Why don't you dress them up as little cupids for the wedding? They're the ones who got Jared and me back together."

"We could hang them from hooks on the church ceiling, and they could flutter overhead during the ceremony," Sam deadpanned.

Lori laughed. "That might be considered child abuse."

"Oh, pooh. They'd probably enjoy it. But wiser heads will prevail."

"Unhook me, will you?" She turned, and Sam performed the honors.

The joy of preparing for a wedding eased the anxiety that had grown since her inexcusable gaffe the previous day. While the disclosure hardly constituted major news, the L.A. press loved celebrity gossip, and Dr. Tartikoff was a celebrity.

In response to the uproar, Jennifer had released a statement saying that the hospital was talking with several distinguished candidates and that nothing had been confirmed. As far as Sam could determine, Dr. T himself remained incommunicado. She hated to think what an uncomfortable situation she'd created for him at his current Boston hospital.

Worst of all, she'd let Mark down. So far, he hadn't said a word to her about it.

Or about anything else.

"Is there a wedding rehearsal?" Sam asked as she helped Lori hang up the beautiful gown on a padded hanger.

"No. Since it's such a small ceremony, the minister offered to tell us what to do right beforehand. I'm just lucky the church was available."

"On a Thursday night? Who'd get married then? I mean, besides you." Sam eased the garment bag over the gown.

"They're booked solid on Friday for New Year's Eve, and on New Year's Day," Lori said. "Some people consider that a lucky time to get married. It was either Thursday or wait until after the first of the year, and we're too impatient."

"Your family must have quite a scramble to come on such short notice." Lori's mother and five sisters lived in Denver.

The bride shook her head. "Only my mom and Louise are coming." That was the next to oldest sister. "The others are tied up with family stuff. They promised to come for the big reception in January."

"I'll look forward to meeting them."

The two women spent the next hour playing with the babies and reviewing plans for decorations and photography, scaled down because of the rush. As Lori noted, she and Jared were saving tons of money, which they'd need for their future children's education.

"You should wait awhile and enjoy each other as a couple," Sam cautioned.

"I agree." Lori knelt on a blanket to change Connie's diaper. "Speaking of couples, what does all this mean for you and Mark? I mean, if he won't even answer your email..."

Sam sighed. "I wish I knew." After the way she'd betrayed his confidence, how could he ever trust her again?

"And what about the clinic? Mrs. Wycliff told you never to darken their doorstep again."

Sam steeled her resolve. "She needs to learn her lesson the hard way."

"What lesson?" Lori returned the baby to the playpen and went into the kitchen to wash her hands.

Since the kitchen opened onto the living room, Sam continued talking. "I'm taking her at her word. Even if it kills me, I'm leaving the clinic to her. Let her find out what it takes to manage the peer counselors, handle emergencies and try to persuade professionals to donate services. Raising money is one thing. Serving as interim director is another. She's unqualified, but she's going to have to discover that for herself."

"You're abandoning the clinic?"

Tears stung at the prospect. Sam blinked them away. "Only temporarily. But I mean it. Hands off."

"You're tough," Lori told her.

"I have to be."

As she cradled Colin on her lap, Sam didn't feel tough. She felt guilty and vulnerable and a bit lost. For once in her life, she didn't have a plan to make things right.

She was almost grateful for Eleanor Wycliff's arrogance. Otherwise, the only person she could be angry with was herself.

BECAUSE CHRISTMAS HAD FALLEN on a Saturday, Monday was considered a holiday, giving most workers a three-day weekend. Mark hadn't scheduled any routine surgeries, which was fortunate, because in between a delivery and an unplanned C-section, he spent most of the morning on the phone.

To members of the press, he issued carefully phrased denials about Dr. Tartikoff. With Eleanor, he listened politely and remained noncommittal as she insisted she was ready to take on the clinic in any and all capacities. As for his sister, she hadn't arrived or called. A couple of times Mark started to dial her number, but each time he pulled back. Let her make the first move. Let her take responsibility.

His least favorite call was from Chandra, who didn't believe in taking holidays, either. In fact, he'd reached her on Sunday and absorbed the brunt of her anger then. It had cooled, somewhat—or rather, hardened.

"I phoned Owen Tartikoff personally," she announced when Mark answered. "He's threatening to withdraw from consideration."

"Only threatening?" That left open a tiny window, which was more than Mark had expected.

"He'll reconsider if you fire Dr. Forrest as chief of pediatrics and remove her hospital privileges."

A lead weight clamped over his chest. "That's outrageous. She's a gifted pediatrician and extremely hardworking. I'm sure she'll be glad to apologize. Privately *and* publicly if he wishes." Judging by Sam's email and text, she appreciated how badly she'd screwed up.

"That's not good enough. She has to go."

He couldn't let a personal relationship influence him on this matter. But Mark considered it his duty to protect his staff, whether that meant Sam or anyone else. "She may have a big mouth, but she hasn't harmed patients or committed any legal or medical errors."

Angry and disappointed as he felt, he saw a vast

difference between his former fiancée's drug theft and Sam's mistake. The first had been calculated and illegal, the second a relatively minor error in judgment.

"She embarrassed us publicly! After the way we botched this, I doubt anyone of his caliber will look twice at the fertility center." Her voice bristled.

To keep the peace, Mark refrained from observing what an exaggeration that was. "Let me talk to Owen myself. I'm sure he'll see things differently once he simmers down." In his experience, people often backed away from ultimatums after a day or so of reflection.

"Simmers down? You're forgetting his reputation."

The man was known for terrorizing nurses and antagonizing coworkers, but Mark had been willing to attribute that to perfectionism. Now, though, doubts bubbled to the surface. Dr. Tartikoff had no business insisting that the hospital fire its head of pediatrics over a verbal blunder. If Owen was that arrogant, he might not be the best choice to head up the new center.

He doubted Chandra would see it that way, however, so he tried a different tack. "Has it occurred to you how it will look if we fire Dr. Forrest under these circumstances? The press will have a field day."

"Then it's your job to persuade her to move on voluntarily," Chandra said. "If she's as outstanding as you say, I'm sure she has plenty of other opportunities."

Sure, but I don't want her to take them. Unthinkable to lose Sam not only as a lover but also as a friend and colleague.

Yet he stopped short of a direct refusal. This position at Safe Harbor had given Mark the chance of a lifetime, to transform a community hospital into a first-rate medical center for women and babies, and the fertility center represented the jewel in the crown. Securing someone of

Tartikoff's stature was critical. Two years ago, Mark had made a major life decision to come here, and he wasn't ready to throw away this opportunity without exploring all options.

"I'll discuss it with her," he said into the phone.

"Do this right, Mark."

That, he reflected as he said goodbye, was exactly the point.

DESPITE THE HOLIDAY, SAM SAW patients on Monday morning because kids always managed to get sick on Christmas. She attributed that to a combination of irregular diet, too little sleep and viruses transmitted from person to person at holiday gatherings.

At midafternoon, she wolfed down a sandwich in the hospital cafeteria. About to head for her office on the fourth floor to catch up on paperwork, she saw Mark sitting alone at a table, watching her.

Glad that there was no one around to snoop and stare and gossip, she joined him. Her heart twisted as this man who normally radiated welcome merely lifted a hand in greeting.

It's my own fault. "I'm sorry," Sam replied miserably.

"I know. I got your messages." His voice rang hollowly through the empty cafeteria. "I was just going to call you."

"Did Tartikoff tell you to jump off a cliff?"

"Not exactly."

She saw the conflict in his eyes. He didn't have to say another word. "I'm the sacrificial lamb. Well, I refuse to be forced out. Honestly, Mark! It's not as if I screwed up a diagnosis or was negligent with a patient!"

"I know that," he said quietly.

"I refuse to accept a blot on my record. Getting fired is

unreasonable, unfair and a violation of my contract. You know perfectly well I could fight this."

He nodded. "No one's firing you."

"What, then?"

"Chandra asked me to persuade you to leave voluntarily. Sam, it's up to you. I'll fight right alongside you if that's what you want."

On the verge of agreeing, she hesitated. She wanted very much to stay. Not for the counseling clinic, which she seemed unable to save, and not for being chief of pediatrics—heck, she might resign from that position, anyway— but for her patients and friends, and to be around Mark. Mostly, to stay with Mark.

Where could this relationship lead, though? They saw the world from such opposite perspectives that something like this had been bound to happen, sooner or later. If she stayed, it would happen again.

Should she consider her other options? Sam had built a comfortable nest in Safe Harbor, but now that she had children, maybe she ought to consider moving closer to family.

"My brother's been trying for ages to talk me into moving back to Seattle," she said.

"He's a cardiologist, isn't he?"

She nodded. "On the other hand, now that I've finally paid off my student loans, I'd prefer to join my parents in Mexico. It would be great for my kids to live near their grandparents."

"You're sure you're okay with this?" His tone implied that *he* wasn't.

Neither was Sam, yet she ought to be feeling enthusiastic. She'd always planned to make a major contribution to the poor, and here was her chance. So what if she'd miss the life she'd established in Safe Harbor? *I owe a debt to those who're suffering.* Her parents were always talking about the need for more doctors.

"It may take me a few months to work out the legalities with adopting the triplets," she warned. "And I also have to find a pediatrician to take over my practice. But I could make an announcement as soon as I talk to my parents. Maybe right after the first of the year."

He scowled. "I hate this. They have no business forcing you out. I'm the one who leaked sensitive information."

"And I'm the one who shot my mouth off, as usual. Besides, I've always intended to do something like this eventually. And I miss my family." That reminded her. "Speaking of family, did your sister ever get here?"

He shook his head. "I'm a little concerned, but I refuse to climb back on that emotional roller coaster. This time, I'll wait for her to contact me." His brow furrowed as he stared past Sam. "Do you realize it's snowing?"

She glanced out the glass doors to the patio. Sure enough, snowflakes were swirling thickly around deserted tables and chairs. "Wow, that's more than a flurry. It's starting to accumulate. But that never happens in southern California."

"Sure it does. Once or twice a decade."

"Special for us." Sam couldn't believe she was feeling sentimental about snow, but their weekend in the mountains would remain a cherished memory all her life.

Mark's mouth curved into a smile. "Snowballs."

"Oh, come on!"

"Dare you."

She couldn't resist following as he went to open the doors. A blast of chilly air raised goose bumps beneath Sam's sweater, but she didn't care.

Outside, white fluff transformed the nearby hedge and the parking lot beyond it into a scene of pristine beauty.

She gazed upward at the unfamiliar sight of snow dusting palm trees.

Crouching by a bush, Mark scraped a thin layer of white into his hands. "Brace yourself."

"Oh, grow up. Just think, we barely missed having a white Christmas. Wouldn't that have been lovely?" Determined not to be outmatched, Sam brushed the snowy accumulation on a tabletop into her own palms and pressed it hard. As soon as she opened her hands, the stuff fell apart. "This won't pack."

"I thought we were supposed to grow up," he reminded her as his own would-be snowball melted in his hand.

"I'll grow up if you will."

Mark tipped his face to the sky. Flakes dappled his dark hair and eyebrows. "I could move to Seattle with you."

"I'm going to Mexico."

"Oh, be a sport. It *never* snows down there."

"Great food, though."

"If you like things spicy."

Sam stopped talking as the snow blotted out the world around them. She loved being isolated with Mark. A week ago, they'd played in the snow and hurried back to the cabin with their arms around each other. If only they could do that again.

Time, stand still. Let me stay here with him.

His cell phone beeped. He glanced at the message. "Delivery."

"I'd better go, too. The paperwork keeps piling up. Whatever made me think I was cut out to be a bureaucrat?" Sam grumbled. "You can replace me as chief of pedes right away. Please."

He slid an arm around her waist. "My pleasure."

"Mark! Anyone can see us."

He kissed the tip of her nose. "Well, they can't accuse

me of favoring you, since I'm about to remove you as chief of pediatrics."

His body sheltered hers, warm against the cold, solid against the fragility of snow. "They'll gossip anyway," she said, and touched her lips to his. Immediately, she wanted more.

He lifted his head. "Who cares?" And he proceeded to kiss her thoroughly. They stood there for a while, wrapped up in each other, until his beeper went off.

"Delivery," they both said.

To be discreet, Sam let him go inside ahead of her. When she entered, she saw only a couple of cafeteria workers, whose positions required them to face away from the patio. Lucky break, she supposed.

Sam didn't feel lucky.

She never ran from a challenge, and that was not her intention now. By leaving Safe Harbor she'd be running *to* the kind of commitment she'd always wanted to make. So why was she listening to a selfish inner voice that urged her to stay?

Better tackle those reports awaiting her attention upstairs. She owed a clean desk and an empty in-basket to whoever succeeded her as chief.

On the way, she decided to stop and see if Mark's secretary had his sister's phone number. There was no harm in checking on Bryn, just to be certain she hadn't run into trouble.

Chapter Seventeen

The snowfall amounted to less than an inch, but that was enough to pass for a blizzard in southern California. Although the stuff melted within an hour, the news media provided coverage of freeway jams, farmers struggling to save their citrus and avocado crops, children frolicking and people using hair dryers to deice their front steps. Safe Harbor's latest snafu seemed to be forgotten—except by those who mattered.

True to her word, Sam informed Mark that she'd put in some phone calls about finding a replacement pediatrician and spoken to Tony about fast-tracking the adoption. However, Mark realized that little could be accomplished during this week between Christmas and New Year's, when half the world had gone out of town.

The situation had almost driven the counseling clinic from his mind, until Eleanor stopped by his office late on Thursday afternoon. "I never thought I'd say this, but would you please tell Dr. Forrest I didn't mean to drive her away entirely?"

"You could speak to her yourself." Mark hated to rush this conversation, but he still had to pick up his tuxedo from the cleaners for Jared and Lori's wedding tonight.

"She scares me."

He regarded the aristocratic woman in her designer suit. "You're kidding."

Her chest heaved. "I suppose I'm having trouble acknowledging how high-handed I was. It never occurred to me that, without her, there truly isn't anyone in charge. Clients show up without appointments, peer counselors go on vacation and don't tell anybody, and there's no one to keep a lid on things. I've had to drive down here two days in a row. This is crazy."

"I'll ask her to pitch in." He felt certain Sam would do her best.

Eleanor drummed her fingers on his desk. "I suppose I was unreasonably optimistic about budgeting and staffing. I doubt we'll be able to afford a real director for at least a year. We need Dr. Forrest."

He took a deep breath. "I'm afraid that, at best, she'll only be around for a few more months." He explained about Sam's decision to relocate.

"Is this because of me?" Eleanor asked in dismay.

"It's a lot of things," he said. "She's always intended to work full-time at a low-cost clinic eventually."

"But she's got three children! Has she any idea what an education costs these days?"

"If I could change her mind, I would." Listening to his own words, Mark realized he meant it. And that he'd accepted her decision to leave much too readily.

He loved Safe Harbor Medical Center and everything he'd accomplished in the past couple of years. Even more, he treasured the prospect of what he planned to accomplish in the years to come.

Yet without Sam, all the flavor went out of the place. He couldn't imagine coming to work every day without looking forward to seeing her. Or going home to his sterile house, knowing he'd never hold her in his arms again.

If he wanted to change Sam's mind, he had to do something drastic. And he'd better do it soon.

The problem was, he had no idea how to accomplish that.

As CO-MAIDS OF HONOR, Sam and Jennifer had been instructed to walk down the aisle side by side. They stood waiting their turn in the church foyer, wearing identical silver-and-blue dresses, Jennifer's dark hair and Sam's blond curls pinned back with matching silvery ornaments. Sam hoped the three-inch difference in their heights didn't look awkward.

Oh, well, who would notice? Lori's auburn splendor and the joy on her face were bound to steal the show.

"Have I apologized enough?" Jennifer asked in a low voice. She and Lori were among the few Sam had told about her decision to leave. "I feel like I helped push you into this."

Sam tried to reassure her friend. "I'm famous for shooting my mouth off. I just did it one time too many." She didn't bother to repeat her contention that she'd always intended either to join her parents in Mexico or work at a similar facility elsewhere. Her closest friends knew that she wouldn't have chosen this particular timing.

Her mom, too, had cautioned her not to make a snap decision. "Not that I wouldn't be thrilled to have you here. Either way, I'm coming to visit my three new grandchildren next month, the first chance I get," she'd added.

The thought of the triplets soothed Sam. They seemed to get stronger and smarter every day. Since they still weren't big enough to sleep through the night, she'd used a referral service to find a nanny who specialized in caring for twins and triplets. Nanny Nancy had started two days ago and was holding down the fort this evening.

Already, she'd organized the house so Sam no longer banged into furniture and tripped over supplies. The woman was capable, cheerful and experienced.

Wonder how she'd feel about moving to Mexico.

The music shifted into their cue. "Don't trip," Jennifer advised.

"I wasn't planning to."

"I'm talking to myself, not you."

"Let's hope neither of us trips," Sam suggested.

"Go!" Lori urged from behind.

Silver bells and green-and-silver wreaths gave the small chapel a wintry charm. In the pews, friendly, familiar faces greeted them. Tony Franco and his fiancée, Kate. Ian Martin and nursing director Betsy Raditch. Doctors and nurses, childbirth educator Tina Torres, secretary May Chong…people who'd become like family over the past five years. How could she leave them?

But she had to. Controversy aside, this was what she'd always meant to do.

Finally, Sam allowed herself to focus on the man standing beside Jared at the altar, studying Sam with a gaze that could melt chocolate. In that crisp tuxedo, Mark Rayburn might have been a Mediterranean prince or an old-time movie star. Or simply the man she loved.

I didn't really admit that, did I?

Her chest tightened as she struggled to come to terms with her sudden romanticism. It must be the effect of walking down an aisle clutching a bouquet, she told herself desperately.

What she should have done was paid more attention to her footing. As she reached the front, she took a misstep, stumbled and might have fallen if Jennifer hadn't grabbed her arm.

"You promised!" her friend hissed.

"Sorry." Regaining her balance, Sam took her place beside her fellow maid of honor. When she glanced over at Mark, she caught the edge of a grin and a small headshake. *Hopeless*, it said.

She didn't have time to dwell on her clumsiness. The wedding march swelled and, along with the guests, Sam turned her attention to Lori. The bride glowed with happiness as she strolled down the aisle on her mother's arm.

Sam's eyes misted as Lori reached Jared and the couple joined hands in front of the minister. Thank goodness these two people hadn't lost each other, because they obviously belonged together.

Sometimes things worked out the way you hoped. And sometimes, she conceded with a pang, they didn't.

SINCE THE COUPLE HADN'T BEEN able to find an affordable facility at the last minute, the cake-and-champagne reception took place in the hospital's workout room, which was also used for childbirth classes. Lori had assured Mark that she didn't mind, since her "real" reception would be held at a restaurant the following month.

Nevertheless, it was hard to ignore the posters detailing the stages of labor, and another graphically depicting exercises for pregnant women. "I think every couple should have posters like these at their reception," joked Tina, the childbirth instructor.

"I didn't realize they were still going to be up," Lori said tartly. "I may deal with pregnancies every day, but on a personal level, I'd rather not think about it for a few years yet."

Jared gave his new wife a hug. "We can start practicing, though, right?"

"For which part?" she challenged.

"You don't expect me to spell it out here, do you, sweetheart?"

As Lori's cheeks flushed, Mark raised his glass. "I propose a toast. To the couple best qualified of anyone I know to practice for childbirth."

Amid the laughter, he saw a wistful expression fleet across Sam's face. Did she still regret losing the chance to experience pregnancy? But what a blessing to have Colin and Connie and Courtney.

She still had the chance to enjoy every step of parenthood. As for Mark, he'd felt thousands of babies move inside their mothers, seen them on ultrasounds, and listened to their heartbeats. He'd never minded that he didn't get to keep any of them.

He minded now. How could he let the triplets grow up without him?

Jennifer appeared at his side. "I just got an alert about a website you ought to see."

"We're both off duty," he protested.

"I still get alerts on my cell phone. This one concerns Dr. Tartikoff."

The name no longer inspired enthusiasm. More like antipathy. "Oh?"

"He's been selected scientist of the year." A prestigious journal had just announced the honor, she explained as she brought up the magazine's website on her phone. Reluctantly, Mark accepted the device and scanned the story, which could only make matters worse as far as the corporate owners were concerned. Now they'd want him more than ever.

A flattering photo made Tartikoff look like a TV star. Mark was less impressed with the interview, in which the doctor went on at great length about the latest developments in manipulating DNA to eliminate genetic diseases.

While he hadn't pioneered the techniques, a reader might get that impression from the way the guy boasted about his stellar record with patients.

Sour grapes on my part. But Mark had to admit he'd still love to have Owen's name attached to the fertility center.

Chandra had told the doctor of Sam's willingness to leave, but so far he'd made no decision. After this coup, Mark supposed offers would flood in from all over the globe. How ironic if they lost Dr. Tartikoff, anyway.

He returned the phone to Jennifer. "That's quite an honor. Thanks for showing it to me."

That night, Mark slept badly. He tossed and kicked off the sheets and felt angry at everyone. *Okay, so Owen's a genius. But who's the administrator of this damn hospital, anyway?*

Mark didn't intend to spend the next few years catering to the fellow's ego or his touchy temperament. Professional respect had to cut both ways. Three ways—to Samantha, as well.

Regardless of her claim that she wanted to join her parents in Mexico, she was being forced out. Taking Mark's joy and sense of purpose with her.

Maybe eventually he'd regain his dedication to the hospital. Maybe he'd find satisfaction in landing an incredibly gifted and innovative surgeon for his staff, whether Dr. Tartikoff or someone else. But it wasn't enough.

By the time he dozed off at last, he'd come to a difficult decision.

Mark spent much of Friday morning making notes on what he wanted to say to Chandra, then deleted all of them. On impulse, he pulled up the website from last night and reread the article. Spotting an option for reader comments, he clicked over to scan them.

Amid a profusion of posts, many lauded Dr. T's accomplishments. Others took a less pleasant tone, including several that accused him of playing God. A nurse who claimed to be a former coworker called him arrogant to the point of cruelty. A former patient contended he'd unsuccessfully pushed her into high-tech procedures, and that, later, another doctor had helped her get pregnant with simpler and less costly techniques.

Suddenly Mark knew what he wanted to say. Not to the corporation vice president, but to Owen himself.

He put in a call, and got the man's voice mail. Too impatient to delay, Mark left a message that might very well end his career at Safe Harbor.

SAM WASN'T SURE WHEN PEOPLE had fallen into the habit of calling the entire day of December 31 "New Year's Eve." As far as she was concerned, the evening didn't begin until after five. To her, Friday was just another workday.

She spent the morning seeing patients, then took her nurse to lunch and broke the news that she might be leaving but would make sure her staff still had jobs.

"I hate—who is it I'm supposed to hate?" Devina demanded. "Who did this?"

"I always planned..."

"Yes, yes, the suffering poor." Her nurse waved a perfectly manicured hand. How she managed to keep those nails beautifully shaped and polished despite the demands of her profession was the subject of speculation among her coworkers. "This is a terrible idea."

"I appreciate your support." Sam waited while a waiter wearing Papa Giovanni's white-and-red-trimmed green uniform refilled her glass.

Devina sniffed a piece of garlic bread and set it aside. An obsessive calorie watcher, she claimed to satisfy her cravings that way. "Dr. Tartikoff should think about which doctor is going to take care of the babies *after* they're born. What does he imagine, that he brings them into the world and they disappear into a cloud of happiness? He's only a small part of their lives."

"I doubt that idea ever pierced his ego." Sam was going to miss her nurse. Just being around Devina lightened her spirits.

"He'd better not cross my path." Her nurse stabbed a single tortellini with her fork. "I hear he reduces his nurses to tears. Huh."

"Good thing you're a pedes nurse so you won't have to work with him."

Devina chewed and swallowed carefully. "Don't leave, Samantha. You belong here."

Sam felt that way, too, even though her higher self told her otherwise.

After lunch, she gave her staff the rest of the day off. In her medical building office, Sam clicked through emails, glad to get this chore out of the way. Once she collected the babies for the holiday, she wanted to devote her full attention to them.

A message from Mark's sister apologized for being short when Sam called earlier in the week. "I'm sorry I was defensive. Like I said, I'll drive out there one of these days and surprise my brother. I spent Christmas with my mentor, dealing with old guilt feelings. I know I let Mark down. I'm really good at that, aren't I? I haven't even worked up the nerve to apologize yet."

"Don't let guilt rule your life," Sam wrote back. "We're all guilty of something. Put it behind you. Happy New Year."

She returned to scrolling. Near the end of the email

queue, a message line caught her eye. "From Artie Ortega's family."

Before she could read it, the phone rang. It was the nursery.

"Your daughters don't seem well," the worker said. "Could you come over and check on them?"

Sam's heart leaped into her throat. "Right away," she said, and instantly forgot everything else.

Chapter Eighteen

Having put his job in jeopardy, Mark did something else uncharacteristic: he left work early on New Year's Eve to go shopping.

There were, he saw as he cruised the residential streets of Safe Harbor, no yard sales on holidays. He did, however, find a thrift store that hadn't closed yet.

Fortified with a couple of purchases, he drove to Sam's house. Before leaving the hospital, he'd learned that she'd taken the triplets home, so he knew she must be there. The day care worker had also mentioned that Connie and Courtney suffered from colds. Good thing they had a pediatrician for a mother.

He parked in front of her bungalow. A strand of colored lights blinked at him flirtatiously, slightly off synch with the neighbor's flashier display.

Mark had no idea when he'd fallen in love with Samantha. But after he left the message for Owen and sat there hoping with all his heart that somehow he'd find a way to keep her on staff, he'd realized the "somehow" wasn't enough.

Well, here he was. Nervous, but too impatient to delay.

He got out of his car. Since he could hear the babies

crying, he didn't have to worry about waking them, so he gave the bell a jab.

"It's open!" called a thick voice that sounded like Samantha's.

Mark cracked open the door to a blast of moist air and the scent of pine. "Hello? It's me."

"Over here." She sat on the couch, her face puffy and red as if from crying. Blond hair straggled every which way, some of it stuck behind her ears, some sweeping over the baby cradled in her arms. Her jogging suit bore splashes of formula.

From an inside room, he heard the other two triplets fussing. While he considered it unlikely that a trio of babies with head colds could have reduced Sam to such a state, Mark didn't stop to quiz her. First things first. "Do the kids have temperatures?"

"Low grade," she told him. "Just the girls."

He set the thrift-store bag on an end table. "Coughing and sneezing?"

"Yes."

"Leave this to me."

Half an hour later, Colin—the easiest of the three to deal with today—was fed, diapered and asleep. Courtney, who'd been in Sam's arms, had also been settled in bed, her congestion eased by saline nose drops and a cool-mist vaporizer.

His specialty might not be pediatrics, but Mark kept up with the latest research and agreed with Sam's decision to avoid over-the-counter medications. These didn't work well and in newborns could have dangerous side effects, such as thinning mucus into fluids that might literally drown a baby.

Sam was feeding the last of the trio a bottle as Mark

settled in a chair. On the Christmas tree, the cherub dolls watched with painted smiles and sad eyes.

"Now tell me what's wrong," he said.

She indicated a wrinkled sheet of paper beside her. When he picked it up, he saw that she'd printed out an email. The subject line mentioned Artie Ortega, the young cancer patient from the Christmas party.

His parents wrote that he had died three days after Christmas.

"Thanks to friends like you, our son had the happiest childhood a little boy could ask for. He was an angel and an inspiration in our lives, and he will be with us always."

Like most doctors, Mark tried to distance himself from the fact that, no matter how much you wanted to heal the world, sometimes you failed. But Artie was twelve years old. It shouldn't happen.

"I'm sorry." He wiped away a tear of his own.

Sam blew into a tissue. "Well, that's my news for the day."

"I have some, too."

She regarded him questioningly.

"I just told Owen Tartikoff…well, I more or less told him where to get off." He swallowed. "I said I'm not running a tyranny that penalizes caring and dedicated physicians like you. I said you may be leaving over this, and that in my opinion, it's as much a blow to this hospital as losing him would be."

She adjusted the baby's bottle. "How'd he react?"

"I have no idea. I had to leave a message." Mark described the comments he'd read on the website and explained, "I reminded him that innovative fertility treatments are bound to generate controversy. Does he really want to work with an administrator who cuts and runs in a storm? Because if he does, he's a fool."

Sam had stopped crying. "Did you clear this with Chandra?"

"Nope." What was the point? No matter what she'd said, he'd have done this anyway.

Her forehead puckered. "That was risky. I don't suppose she'd fire you but…"

"I don't care if she does."

"Liar!"

He refused to worry about that. Besides, he had other, more pressing business to deal with. "Do you realize nobody holds yard sales on New Year's Eve? How inconvenient."

She set down the bottle. "Why do you care? You won the bet about your sister."

"But I never collected my kiss. So I figured *one* of us ought to come out ahead." Before she could question his logic, he fished his purchase from the bag and handed it to her. "How's this?"

With an air of wonder, she held up the glass candy dish shaped like a swan and studied the light filtering through the shades of blue. "It's lovely. Thank you."

"It's only a reproduction, according to the clerk," Mark said. "She mentioned something called Depression glass. I was too embarrassed to admit I had no idea what that is." Since Sam was having trouble manipulating both baby and bowl, he transferred the blanket to his shoulder and lifted Connie gently.

"During the Great Depression, companies used to give away cheap glassware to lure buyers," Sam explained. "Manufacturers put pieces in boxes of cereal, and movie theaters handed them out to ticket buyers. They've become popular with collectors." From the center of the bowl, she removed a small item wrapped in newspaper. "What's this?"

"Open it." His hands prickled.

From the paper, she plucked a rainbow-hued glass ring. "This is beautiful. What's it for?"

Now, Mark. "Will you marry me?"

Sam regarded him questioningly. "Are you serious?"

"I love you. Whatever we're doing and wherever we're going, let's do it together. Our future shouldn't depend on other people's decisions." He couldn't put it any more plainly than that.

She gave him a wry, tender smile. "I never pictured myself getting a proposal wearing old sweats covered with baby spit-up."

"I hope that's a yes," Mark said.

When she shook her head, his heart squeezed. "I can't do this to you. Mark, you'd never be happy working at a small clinic."

He refused to give in, because he knew, more certainly than he'd ever known anything, that getting married was the right course for them both. "Just say yes and we'll figure out the details later."

Sam sank back against the cushions. "I'm in no condition to give you an answer right now. Can you be patient with me?"

"Of course." After a beat, he added, "For how long?"

"That's your idea of being patient?"

"You love me. Admit it."

Sam's gaze fell on the email. She stroked the paper lightly. "Tell me something I don't understand. Why did he die and I lived?"

She must be thinking of her own battle with cancer, Mark realized. "You mean, when you were a kid?"

She nodded. "I made friends in the cancer ward. A girl a few years older than me, and a boy about Artie's age.

We'd buck each other up. Joke about our bald heads. Plan reunions for when we got better."

She didn't have to spell it out. "Both of them died?"

"The same week." Fresh tears dampened her cheeks. "I nearly gave up. I *did* give up. I went to bed and cried for days. I got mad at God, and felt sorry for myself, and missed my friends. It was all so wrong. Ironically, my own treatment was going well, but why did I deserve that?"

"Survivor's guilt." Mark had run across the syndrome in his practice. Patients who'd lost loved ones, even in circumstances where they were blameless, sometimes questioned why they deserved to live.

"My mom pulled me out of it," Sam continued. "She sat on the edge of the bed and told me I'd been spared for a reason. That I had the gift of healing. While I was always patching up animals and giving first-aid to my friends, I hadn't been sure I could handle medical school. After that day, I had no doubt. I was spared so I could save other lives."

"And you'll go right on doing that," Mark said. "Wherever you decide to practice."

Sam clutched the paper. "I've been far luckier than I deserve. Yes, it was a blow learning about early menopause, but then I was handed these wonderful babies. I can't go on being selfish, indulging in a cozy job, a comfortable income, a nice house. I have to remember why I was kept alive."

"Marrying me does not amount to thumbing your nose at fate," Mark countered.

She gazed at him tearily. "You're the most wonderful man I've ever met, but living my way would make you miserable."

He disagreed with every cell in his body. On the other

hand, she'd been right about being in no condition to make a life-changing commitment.

"Give the idea a chance to sink in. We'll talk about this later." Since Connie had started squirming in his arms, Mark went and put the baby in her cradle. He paused to watch the three little ones sleeping, their breathing steady against the hum of the vaporizer. *I'm not letting you go. Or your mom, either.*

Standing there, he asked himself a hard question: Was he prepared to move to Mexico to keep them? Could he give up the joy of running a hospital, of building new programs for the future, of harnessing the latest technology? Could he spend his days treating ailments in a struggling clinic, and his nights living in near-poverty?

Maybe for a while. But after that?

Marriage required finding a way to keep them both happy. Sam was right about that.

Well, this was New Year's Eve. In a new year, all things were possible.

He went and broke a twig off the Christmas tree. "What's that for?" Sam asked sleepily.

"My prize. It's not exactly mistletoe, but it's close enough." Holding it above her head, he sat on the couch and claimed his kiss.

THE MONDAY AFTER NEW YEAR'S was a holiday, and, of course, Mark went to the hospital anyway. Delivered babies, cheered the staff members who had to work and stewed about his inability to nail down Sam's agreement to marry him.

They'd spent the weekend together and walked to work today, taking turns pushing the babies in a double-decker triplet pram that her brother had sent for Christmas. To his amusement, they'd spotted some yard sale signs but there hadn't been time to do more than glance at the objects displayed on tables and blankets. In any case, he'd glimpsed nothing much in the way of glassware.

"I do plan to buy a real ring, you know," he'd commented to Sam as they approached the medical center.

"That isn't the issue, Mark. As you well know, you big gorgeous lug." She'd kissed him, and never mind who might see. He rather regretted the discovery afterward that there hadn't been any witnesses.

Today, he wouldn't at all mind stirring up a bit of scandal. Mark the peacemaker, Mark the master of the artful compromise, really wanted to take a poke at somebody. He just had to figure out who.

Certainly not the woman who walked into his office early that afternoon. A tuft of pure white had replaced the sprinkling of gray in his sister's dark hair, but her skin had a healthy glow and her tremulous smile revealed teeth a lot whiter than when he'd last seen her.

"Sorry I'm late," Bryn said.

THAT MORNING, THERE WAS ONLY a trickle of patients. Sam used the extra time to clear out old papers that had accumulated in her desk drawers. Then, eating a sandwich at her desk, she started riffling through the box of holiday cards. Once she finished with each, she set it aside for children's craft projects at the day care center.

As always, the notes and photos warmed her. A gawky boy she'd treated for severe acne stood proudly in his high school graduation robes, his skin clear. His mother thanked Sam for referring him to a dermatologist. "I didn't know it then, but he was so depressed he'd considered suicide," she wrote. "Until you told us, I had no idea that medication might cure him. Thank you from the bottom of my heart."

A bad complexion might not pose as dramatic a threat as cancer, Sam mused, but it could have a profound effect on the patient. Tucking the note into a personal file of keepers, she read on.

"SAM CALLED YOU?" MARK ASKED as he absorbed his sister's explanation that she'd spent Christmas with her mentor, fighting feelings of despair and self-loathing.

"Dr. Forrest told me to stop letting guilt run my life. Which is basically what my mentor said, but somehow it felt different, coming from a friend of yours." Bryn faced him across a cafeteria table after a late lunch.

"That's interesting, considering that Sam lets guilt run *her* life," Mark observed drily. But since he didn't feel right discussing Sam's issues with Bryn, he said, "I still don't understand why you didn't email or call."

"Oh, Mark." When she shook her head, crystal earrings flashed. She'd loaded on the costume jewelry, an effect their mother would have dismissed as gaudy. Now that he'd developed an appreciation for Depression glass, however, he enjoyed the glitter. "You have no idea how intimidating you are."

"Me?" That didn't fit his image of himself. "I never yelled at you, did I?"

"You didn't have to," his sister said ruefully. "I hated hearing that cranky edge to your voice. I felt like, if I ever pushed you hard enough, you might explode."

"Maybe I should have exploded more often," Mark mused. "Would that have helped?"

"Nothing would have helped." Bryn's mouth twisted ironically. "I had to do this on my own, one step at a time."

"Apparently you've succeeded," he said with approval.

"I'm an alcoholic. I'll always have to be careful." She

paused as a couple of nurses, sauntering past with their trays, paused to greet Mark.

He made introductions and was grateful that they didn't linger. Once he and Bryn were alone, he picked up the thread of the conversation. "You're right. There's no cure for addiction, but it can be controlled."

"Coming here is a big step," she admitted. "I want you to understand how sorry I am for what I put you through. You're the best friend I ever had. You cared more about me than anyone, maybe even our parents. And I repaid you by acting like a jerk."

"I forgive you." Now that she sat in front him, this woman he remembered through so many stages of her childhood and adolescence, he felt only gratitude for her recovery.

"Do you really?"

"To prove it, I'm going to take the rest of the day off. You said you don't have to leave till tomorrow morning, right?" He had an idea how they might celebrate their reunion.

She nodded. "I worked New Year's Eve, so I get an extra day off."

"You used to enjoy playing laser tag," he recalled.

"Still do."

"Well?" he said. "What're we waiting for?" Then he added, "There is one stop I'd like to make on the way."

"I hope it's to meet Samantha."

"You're way ahead of me."

SAM WAS BARELY HALFWAY through the accumulation of cards when Mark stopped by to make introductions. She immediately liked his sister's straightforward manner. In Sam's experience, people who'd come to terms with their own failings didn't waste energy on pretenses. They simply accepted others as they had learned to accept themselves.

"I hope I'm not interrupting any plans you guys had for this evening," Bryn told her. "We could all get together if you like."

"With three screaming infants?" This was Nanny Nancy's night off. "I'll let you enjoy your evening together." Mark had explained that Bryn planned to drive back to Phoenix first thing tomorrow.

"Thanks." He gave Sam a look full of tenderness. "For encouraging Bryn to contact me and for that excellent advice you gave her."

She wasn't sure what he meant. "Advice?"

"About guilt." He left it at that and guided his sister toward the door.

"I hope I get a chance to know you better," Bryn added. "Next visit, okay?"

"Absolutely." *But it had better come in the next month or so, because after that I'll be gone.*

Sam's chest tightened at the thought. Despite her attempts to whip up some enthusiasm, she hated the idea of leaving Safe Harbor.

If she married Mark, Bryn would be her sister-in-law. Sam pictured them all gathered around his living room or at the cabin, laughing as the triplets toddled and plopped on the floor.

No. Erase that image.

She'd be somewhere else, doing what she was meant to do. After all, how many people were lucky enough to have a mission in life as significant as hers?

Wistfully, she went back to reading, but didn't get far before her phone rang. "Dr. Forrest."

In the split second before the caller replied, she heard

a girl's voice in the background say, "Mom! Quit eating all the fudge."

"I'm only testing it" came a crisp voice. "Sorry. This is Eleanor Wycliff."

"Happy New Year." That seemed a civil greeting, which was the best Sam could do. She and Eleanor hadn't crossed paths since their fencing match in the media a week earlier.

"Mark told me that you're leaving and I think it's ridiculous. Please stay. I hope you'll continue as the clinic's adviser, too. We need you."

"I'm sorry—I can't," Sam said.

A long sigh. "I was afraid you'd say that, but I hoped..." Eleanor broke off, and in the background Sam heard her daughter say, "Tell her about Vivien."

"What about Vivien?" Sam asked.

Eleanor gave a dry chuckle. "I stopped by the shelter to see Mrs. Babcock and apologize for being rude to her. I won't say that I like her, but she's much more tolerable when she's sober. Thanks for showing me that even people who lack social skills deserve sympathy."

"You're welcome." If Eleanor was mature enough to apologize for her mistakes, the clinic wasn't in such bad hands after all.

"Now, I have another request. If you insist on leaving, at least keep guiding us long-distance. Answer our questions and keep us focused on why the clinic was established in the first place."

Sam's mood lifted at the notion that she didn't have to give up all contact with the project. "I'd be happy to consult by phone or email."

"That's wonderful."

"Remember the slogan" came Libby's voice over the clang of a pot.

"Watch where you put that, dear!" her mother said. Back to Sam, she explained, "We've decided we need a slogan. Something to keep the staff, volunteers and clients in a positive frame of mind. Any ideas?"

A slogan? "That's more Jennifer's area than mine."

"She suggested Optimism in the face of adversity, then shortened it to, Think positive, but I'd prefer something with more snap."

"I'll let it simmer in my brain." Perhaps one of the cards would provide inspiration.

After the call, pleased to have made peace with Eleanor, Sam resumed reading. A young mother thanked her for a referral to counseling to treat her depression. She also heard from a girl with curvature of the spine, who now stood straight and was training to become a dancer. A mother wrote that her autistic son, referred for early intervention, had improved enough by age five to enroll in a regular kindergarten.

By the time she finished, Sam ached with longing to stay here in this place where she'd done so much good. But her higher and better self responded with a resounding "no."

Although it was only midafternoon, she felt too restless to linger. Pushing the stroller home through the crisp air ought to clear her mind and perhaps help her come up with a slogan for Eleanor.

If not, at least she could stop at yard sales and indulge in a little shopping.

Chapter Nineteen

Mark's urge to give someone a sharp poke, which had gone into hibernation during his sister's visit, came roaring back early Tuesday morning when he realized Owen Tartikoff still hadn't returned his call. Annoyed, he dialed the man's number in Boston.

"Tartikoff," came the curt response.

"This is Mark Rayburn. In case you didn't get my message…"

"I got it," the man said. "Let me be sure I understand correctly. You consider Dr. Forrest as much an asset to Safe Harbor as I would be."

"That's about the size of it."

"I'll take the job."

Having braced for an argument, Mark tried to make sense of Owen's words. "You're accepting the position as director of the fertility center?"

"Unless you've changed your mind about offering it to me."

"Welcome aboard." Mark struggled to bring his reaction in line with this unexpected development. "When can you start?"

"I have a contract to fulfill here, so I won't be able to come full-time until next summer. But we can get started implementing policy." As they agreed on a timetable, Mark wondered whether to ask what had influenced Owen's decision. The new director saved him the trouble. "I admire a man or woman who can stand up to me. In the long run, it leads to better outcomes. I look forward to working with you and to meeting this fire-breathing pediatrician."

"We're excited to have you join us." Mark decided against mentioning that Sam seemed resolved to leave. Or that he, too, might depart.

"Shall I give Ms. Yashimoto a call with my decision?" the fertility specialist asked.

"I'll handle that." Mark had a piece of business to settle with Chandra, as well. After a bit more discussion with Owen, he put through a call to the vice president and, when she answered, broke the news about Tartikoff.

"That's fantastic!" Her voice registered relief. "How on earth did you pull this off?"

"I stood up to him," Mark said. "And that's the second reason I'm calling you. It's about the chain of command."

"Excuse me?"

"You shouldn't have called him in the first place. The corporation hired me as hospital administrator, and that means I'm the person Owen reports to. I don't want him going over my head every time there's a disagreement."

A long silence greeted his remarks. Finally, she said, "I didn't mean to undercut your authority, but this project is of the utmost importance."

"I thought the hospital as a whole was of the utmost importance," he answered coolly. "*Including* the fertility center."

"Well, of course."

Might as well go for broke. "I should warn you that I'm considering leaving when Dr. Forrest does. She and I may be taking on a new challenge together." That was a stretch, since Sam hadn't agreed to any such thing, but Mark was in no mood to pull his punches.

Chandra gasped. "Mark, we can't afford to lose you."

"I suspect that's an exaggeration." He'd expended far too much energy these past months mediating between Chandra and his staff—Sam in particular—to fall for idle compliments.

"You have no idea what a brilliant job you're doing. Safe Harbor is our flagship hospital. One of our other hospitals is in bad shape due to poor leadership, and a couple of others are struggling. You're even more important to us than Dr. Tartikoff." Chandra spoke in a rush, with no sign of her usual calculation. "I hope you'll reconsider, Mark. And Dr. Forrest, as well. We'd like for her to stay in any capacity you deem fit."

Hmm. Interesting. "I'll take that into consideration."

"Naturally we'll be raising both your salaries by ten percent," Chandra added.

Even more interesting. "Much appreciated. I'll get back to you soon."

After hanging up, Mark sat staring out the window toward the harbor. He loved this view and he'd really hate to abandon it.

Now for the tough part: persuading Sam to stay.

A tap at the door ushered in Eleanor Wycliff. "Good morning," she said, far too cheerily for someone who'd presumably driven all the way from Beverly Hills in what he'd heard on the radio was heavy postholiday traffic. "How do you like the clinic's new slogan?" She indicated a bright yellow lapel button bearing a prominent single word: Yes!

"Excellent." Mark tried to show more interest than he felt. Right now the clinic was the least of his concerns.

"Dr. Forrest found a box of them at a yard sale

yesterday," Eleanor continued. "Well, I won't keep you. Ciao!"

After she'd gone, he reflected on the fact that he and Sam had been offered substantial raises. What a shame to give those up. Still, she'd never let money influence her decision.

He was marshalling his arguments when Lori popped in. "Just a reminder that you have patients scheduled this morning."

Mark checked his watch. "In half an hour. I'm aware of that, thanks."

She tapped her own Yes! button. "I like the clinic's new slogan so much, I thought I'd wear one, too."

"I hope you sanitized it. I understand they came from a yard sale."

"Grouch." Quickly, she added, "Yes, I did."

Something occurred to Mark. "Wait a minute. Shouldn't you be on your honeymoon?"

"Jared couldn't reschedule his duties on such short notice, so we took a long weekend in Palm Springs," the nurse answered. "Anyway, I wouldn't miss this."

"Miss what?"

She gave him a broad smile and ducked out. He imagined her grin still hanging in midair, as if she were the Cheshire cat.

What was going on?

Then Sam came in. "Hi." She pointed to her yellow Yes! button.

"Good morning." Mark took a deep breath. "I have good news."

"Oh?" She quirked one of her amazing eyebrows. The gesture seemed to convey a world of meaning, but at the moment, he had no idea what it was.

"Dr. Tartikoff's going to be joining our staff. Also,

Chandra wants you to stay at Safe Harbor and she's offered us both ten percent raises."

"What's the punch line?" Sam asked. She looked particularly lovely today, he observed, with her hair curling seductively around the shoulders of her tweed suit. He'd missed walking to work with her this morning, but he'd wanted to have breakfast with Bryn.

"No punch line. I'm serious."

"Good thing." She indicated her button again.

"I like the new slogan," Mark said politely.

"It's also the answer to your question."

Which question? "Refresh my memory."

She held up her left hand. The rainbow ring, adapted to fit with a thick Band-Aid, clung to her third finger. "That question."

When Mark started to rise, his knees defied him, and he sank down again. "You'll marry me?"

"I love you. Whatever we're doing and wherever we're going, let's do it together."

"That's the most brilliant thing I ever heard." This time, he propelled himself upright and strode around the desk.

"Actually, you said it." Sam reached for him. "I was quoting you."

"I did? I must be a genius." He gathered her in his arms, exactly where she belonged.

"I finally figured out," she murmured, "that I shouldn't let defying death take over my life."

"You're a genius, too."

"And since you'd be monstrously unhappy in a small clinic, I've decided to stay here." She nuzzled the curve of his throat. "As long as I'm getting a ten percent raise."

Mark breathed in the scent of baby powder and peppermint. A practical woman, his future wife. "I'm glad you dressed for the occasion, by the way. You're smashing."

"I had to erase that image of myself receiving a proposal in sweats and baby spit-up."

He wanted to be sure she wouldn't regret this. "What about that dream of yours? The idea that you were saved for a reason?"

"I still believe that," Sam replied. "The thing is, I kept saying no to my own instincts. After I bought these buttons, I felt them nagging at me all night. Finally I got the message about saying yes. That I can save the world one child at a time just as well right here in Safe Harbor."

Mark kissed her for a very long while. Not as long as he'd have liked, though, because he heard giggling and whispering in the outer office. Reluctantly, he lifted his head. "What now?"

Catching his hand in hers, Sam stepped back and called out, "Okay, guys."

Lori entered first, with Eleanor and Jennifer right behind. "Can we pop the champagne now?" his nurse asked. "It's really sparkling apple juice."

"Please do." As Eleanor twisted off the lid, Mark didn't even mind that Sam had told her friends about her decision before she'd told him. Otherwise, how could she have arranged this celebration?

"I had my fingers crossed for you both," Jennifer added.

"Was there any doubt about how I'd react?" Mark had already proposed, after all.

Lori poured juice carefully into plastic champagne flutes. "With the two of you, we never can tell."

Come to think of it, neither could he.

ON A BALMY MORNING IN February, Dr. Mark Rayburn and Dr. Samantha Forrest set out on foot from their large home on a cul-de-sac. While he lowered the oversize stroller to the walkway, she locked the door on the once-austere house, which seemed much friendlier now that it was stuffed with a flowery sofa and chairs, baby furniture and a collection of colored glassware.

Dr. Rayburn and Dr. Forrest, who had discussed merging their names when they said their vows but decided Rayburn-Forrest would be too much of a mouthful, enjoyed the salty breeze that blew from the ocean and the early spring flowering of pansies, snapdragons and primroses in the yards they passed.

A couple of times, they stopped to tug a blanket into place over one of the triplets, who were getting feistier every day, much like their parents. And occasionally the two doctors' voices rang out in cheerful disagreement about some policy or other. But when they neared the complex, their steps quickened as they eagerly anticipated their arrival at Safe Harbor Medical Center.

This was—and for a very long time into the future would surely remain—*their* hospital.

* * * * *

Watch for the next book in Jacqueline Diamond's
SAFE HARBOR MEDICAL *miniseries—*
OFFICER DADDY—coming soon!

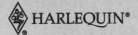
HARLEQUIN®

COMING NEXT MONTH

Available January 11, 2011

#1337 COLORADO COWBOY
American Romance's Men of the West
C.C. Coburn

#1338 RAMONA AND THE RENEGADE
Forever, Texas
Marie Ferrarella

#1339 THE BACHELOR RANGER
Creature Comforts
Rebecca Winters

#1340 THE WEDDING BARGAIN
Here Comes the Bride
Lee McKenzie

HARLEQUIN®

A *Romance*

FOR EVERY MOOD™

Spotlight on

Classic

Quintessential, modern love stories
that are romance at its finest.

See the next page
to enjoy a sneak peek from
the Harlequin Presents® series.

Harlequin Presents® is thrilled
to introduce the first installment of
an epic tale of passion and drama by
USA TODAY *Bestselling Author*
Penny Jordan!

*When buttoned-up Giselle first meets
the devastatingly handsome Saul Parenti,
the heat between them is explosive....*

"LET ME GET THIS STRAIGHT. Are you actually suggesting that I would stoop to that kind of game playing?"

Saul came out from behind his desk and walked toward her. Giselle could smell his hot male scent and it was making her dizzy, igniting a low, dull, pulsing ache that was taking over her whole body.

Giselle defended her suspicions. "You don't want me here."

"No," Saul agreed, "I don't."

And then he did what he had sworn he would not do, cursing himself beneath his breath as he reached for her, pulling her fiercely into his arms and kissing her with all the pent-up fury she had aroused in him from the moment he had first seen her.

Giselle certainly *wanted* to resist him. But the hand she raised to push him away developed a will of its own and was sliding along his bare arm beneath the sleeve of his shirt, and the body that should have been arching away from him was instead melting into him.

Beneath the pressure of his kiss he could feel and taste her gasp of undeniable response to him. He wanted to devour her, take her and drive them both until they were equally satiated—even whilst the anger within him that she should make him feel that way roared and burned its resentment of his need.

She was helpless, Giselle recognized, totally unable to withstand the storm lashing at her, able only to cling to the man who was the cause of it and pray that she would survive.

Somewhere else in the building a door banged. The sound exploded into the sensual tension that had enclosed them, driving them apart. Saul's chest was rising and falling as he fought for control; Giselle's whole body was trembling.

Without a word she turned and ran.

Find out what happens when Saul and Giselle succumb to their irresistible desire in

THE RELUCTANT SURRENDER

Available January 2011 from Harlequin Presents®

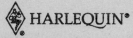

HARLEQUIN®

American ★ Romance®

C.C. COBURN
Colorado Cowboy

American Romance's
Men of the West

It had been fifteen years since Luke O'Malley,
divorced father of three, last saw his high school
sweetheart, Megan Montgomery. Luke is shocked to
discover they have a son, Cody, a rebellious teen on his
way to juvenile detention. The last thing either of them
expected was nuptials. Will these strangers rekindle
their love or is the past too far behind them?

**Available January
wherever books are sold.**

"LOVE, HOME & HAPPINESS"